Other books by Jack Ketchum:

OLD FLAMES
TRIAGE (Anthology)
OFFSPRING
OFF SEASON
THE GIRL NEXT DOOR
SHE WAKES
PEACEABLE KINGDOM
RED
THE LOST

OFFSPRING

JACK KETCHUM

Published by 47North
P.O. Box 400818
Las Vegas, NV 89140

ISBN-13: 9781477806227
ISBN-10: 1477806229

∼

PART I

MAY 12, 1992

12:25 A.M.

She stood dappled in grime and moonlight beneath the drifting branches of the shade tree and watched through the window. Behind her the others jittered.

She touched the screen with her fingertips. It was loose. Old. She rubbed her thumb and forefinger together, felt the fine grit of rust.

She concentrated on the girl inside. The acid-flower scent of her, riding high and strong over the musty-smelling couch on which she lay—even above the warm, grease-soaked kernels of grain in the bowl beside her.

The girl smelled of musk. Of urine and wildflowers.

The girl had breasts and long, dark hair.

Older than she was.

Her clothes were tight.

They would hinder.

The males pressed close, anxious to see. She let them. It was important that they know what lay inside,

3

though she would guide them when the time came. The males were younger and needed guidance.

But this was new to them, and thrilling. The lash of thin birch sticks across their bodies. For balance they would have to look carefully now.

She felt the diamond brush her chest, its cool gold setting, swaying from the dirty knotted twine.

The night was still. Crickets calling in the hollow.

They watched the girl lost and deaf to them in the bright splash of voices out of the flickering light. And each, for a moment, as though brushed with the wind of one sudden mind, felt the baby asleep and alone above them in the thirsty dark—their *dark, the dark of their elders, of the Woman and First Stolen.*

They imagined they could see the child, smell the child.

They only had to watch.

A single cloud had only to pass before the moon.

4

1:46 A.M.

Dammit, Nancy!

Every light in the house was on again. Downstairs, anyway.

She turned the Buick wagon up into the drive.

Girl must think I'm made of money, she thought. *I bet the stereo's on and the TV too and there's no Coke left in the refrigerator.*

She was just a little drunk.

Her right rear wheel slid over the row of rocks and gravel and crushed three of the remaining tulips trying to survive at the edge of the lawn. *To hell with 'em,* she thought.

She'd crushed them sober too, half as often as not.

She cut the motor. Switched off the lights.

She sat there a moment thinking about Dean across the bar, ignoring her, drinking his Wild Turkey, her goddamn *husband* for god's sake looking right through her as though she were a ghost.

5

But that was Dean. Either you got nothing or else you got a whole lot more than you'd ever want to bargain for.

The nothing was better.

It was humiliating, though. And typical. Whether you lived with him or without him he was Mr. Humiliation. He got his kicks that way.

She took a deep breath to shake off the anger and opened the car door, reached for her old black purse with the .32 revolver in the zippered side pocket that she kept there just in case he tried to beat the shit out of her again like he had in the Caribou lot last Friday night, pushed away from the wheel, and got out. It was harder than it should have been. She'd never lost the weight after the baby. She guessed the beers didn't help any. The purse felt heavy on her arm.

Fucking Dean.

She slammed the car door. It didn't shut right on the driver's side. *I got to fix that,* she thought.

With what?

With Dean gone there was hardly enough money to feed her and the baby. That and pay the sitter one night a week. With the housework and the job, that one night a week—a movie and a couple of drinks, maybe—was a necessity now that the baby was finally old enough to be left for a while. But a barmaid made next to nothing in Dead River, and nobody tipped worth a shit. Whatever you had to say about the tourists, they tipped at least.

One more month, she thought, *till tourist season. You just got to hang in there.*

She stepped across the cracked macadam to the

side door, sorting through her key ring for the house key.

She heard something thump through the open kitchen window. A Coke bottle, probably, against the too-expensive butcher-block table. Nancy eating and drinking her out of house and home again.

I guess I could cut down on the beers, she thought. *I could do that. Save a little money that way. I mean, what's important, anyway?*

Me and the baby, right?

She felt a flush of guilt.

Why did she always call her the baby?

Her name was Suzannah. Suzi. It wasn't always *the baby.* She remembered a time when she'd crooned the name. Now she hardly used it. It was as though the baby were just some sort of *thing,* another something in the way like the mortgage on the house and repairs on the roof or the faucet leaking down in the cellar.

She guessed Dean had screwed the pooch on that for her too. Like everything else.

For a moment she could almost cry.

She walked up the stairs and fit the key in the lock.

God *dammit,* Nancy!

She didn't need the key. The door was open.

She'd told the girl again and again—*keep it locked.*

Okay—so Dean was at the bar tonight. But he wasn't *always* going to be. He was going to drop by one of these nights when she wasn't home, when her car wasn't there in the driveway. And twice already he'd threatened to clean her out. Pull up in Walchinski's truck and haul away everything but the dirty laundry.

7

I wouldn't put it past him, she thought.

I got to talk to this girl.

"Nancy?"

She opened the door to the dayroom where the television was on without the sound—whatever goddamn good *that* was—and closed the door behind her and locked it. She kept on walking toward the kitchen. And the first thing she saw was the puddle on the linoleum floor seeping around the corner into the good hardwood floor of the dayroom—Coke, she guessed, coffee, something dark and flowing and *jesus!* she was going to *murder* this girl—and stepping carefully to avoid it, she looked up and at the same time smelled the stink and suddenly what she was going to say froze inside her and so did the scream, so she could only stand there a moment trying to wrench it all into her at once like a single labored breath in a gale-force wind.

Two of them perched on the counter by the sink. Squatting, staring at her, eyes unnaturally bright. Their dangling arms covered with blood.

Children.

While Nancy lay naked on the butcher-block table.

Her body motionless. Pale.

Her arms already gone.

Her clothes lay scattered across the room. Her jeans beside the table—wet, brown and gleaming.

The cabinets were open, boxes and jars broken. Flour, bread crumbs, crackers, sugar, jams and jellies spilled across the counter to the floor.

Her arms were drying in the sink. Along with the dishes.

All this she saw in a moment, saw too that they were

ready for her while her stomach boiled and the girl with the bloody hatchet and the two identical, filthy boys who had been holding Nancy's legs apart turned to her all serious and businesslike and not at all like the younger two squatting grinning on the counter.

She looked at the girl and, empty eyed, the girl looked back, and each seemed to recognize the other and what her presence meant here—and for a moment the object of their thoughts was the same, simultaneous, though the thoughts themselves were as different as blood and stone. The girl's thoughts cold, formal, almost ritualistic, an assertion of power, concerned that this woman should know everything that had happened here. Hers so suddenly urgent and up from so wrenchingly deep inside her that when her daughter's name swelled across her lips

("*Suzannah!*")

she knew Dean had done nothing to change what lay between mother and daughter, it was only a kind of exhaustion of her hopes, temporary, and that given time it would have passed. And knowing this, and knowing that there was no time, she felt her heart break then and there. So that when the smallest boy, the one she hadn't seen before, stepped out from behind the table with the white plastic trash bag pulled tight over the small, still, familiar form inside and held it up to her for her to see, she was already tearing at her purse for the revolver so she could blast them back to whatever hell they came from—and would have—had not the hatchet fallen in its fine arc to the center of her forehead and brought her instantly shuddering to her knees.

Blind to heartbreak forever.

3:36 A.M.

George Peters dreamed that Mary, his wife—dead three years now—had given birth to a son.

Their son was two years old and playing on the floor.

There were wooden blocks all around him and toy trains ran on a track that began beneath the Christmas tree and disappeared down the hall into the Peters' bedroom, returning, somehow, right through the living room window.

Peters was sitting in an armchair reading the paper. It was a bright sunny day in May or June but the Christmas tree was there and the trains ran round and round.

Mary was out visiting. Peters was minding the boy.

Then someone was knocking on the door, urgent. Calling his name.

He got up and it was Sam Shearing, dead *eleven*

11

years now, telling him he had to get the hell out of there, he had to get out of there *now,* he had to grab the boy and run because the train was coming.

Peters told him he knew the train was coming. The train went round and round.

You don't understand! said Shearing. *You don't fucking understand!* And he started to run. Which wasn't like Sam Shearing at all.

Peters blinked and Sam was gone. He closed the door and went back to the living room where the boy was playing, banging his blocks together.

Which was when he heard the train.

Rumbling, barreling toward the house.

Peters snatched up his son. He ran past the tree into the kitchen—a younger Peters, *fast*—while the engine smashed through the living room window and burst across the room, coming at them faster than any man could run, the boy hysterical in his arms and the huge black head of the thing ramming past refrigerator and dishwasher . . .

Bearing down . . .

He woke and it was as though he *had* been running, his ticker was beating so fast. He was sweating. The sheets were wet and smelled of old, stale scotch.

At least there was no headache. He'd remembered the aspirin, for a change. But sitting up his brain felt foggy. He guessed the booze was still working in him.

He looked at the clock. It wasn't even four in the morning. He'd never get back to sleep now.

And sleep was what the scotch was supposed to be about in the first place.

Mary wouldn't have approved, but she would have understood. There was only so much thinking and so much loneliness you were supposed to be asked to handle. Since she died it wasn't just the nightmares that got to him, that made him want to start drinking at four in the afternoon and keep on drinking right on into the night, it was the simple fact of living in the house without her.

Retirement with your best and oldest friend was one thing. Retirement *period* was another.

He heard the knocking again. But it wasn't in the dream this time, it was at his door. And he guessed the other had been that, too. *Insistent.*

"I'm coming! Hold your horses!"

He got up from the bed. A naked old man with a belly.

He went to the dresser for his shorts and to the closet for his pants. Whoever it was had heard him, because the knocking stopped.

But who the hell was coming after him at a quarter to four in the morning? Friends, drinking buddies— they were few and far between now. Half of them dead, half just moved away.

Dead River was almost all strangers these days.

And there he was again. Feeling sorry for himself.

Whiner, he thought.

He had a brother in Sarasota who kept telling him about the good life down there. He and his wife lived in a mobile-home park with a windmill out in front about a mile from Siesta Key. He'd visited once and one thing was sure, they weren't lonely. People dropped by day and night. There was a lot of walking

13

JACK KETCHUM

and bike riding going on, people with heart conditions or circulatory conditions or whatever out getting some exercise, and folks would see his brother and sister-in-law sitting in the shade of the screened-in porch and come on in for a beer.

They went to dances, played golf, went out to restaurants and clubhouses, ran social affairs and potluck dinners.

It wasn't for him.

There was the heat for one thing.

He was a man who liked his seasons. The bare trees in January and the green in May. Even the winter, the way the cold could take your breath away mornings, the shoveling that steamed you up inside your clothes and the wood fires in the grate.

What you had in Florida was just heat. Heat that was fine and pleasant about a third of the time, a little uncomfortable about a third of the time, and a third of the time like walking through steam. Like walking through clouds of your own sweat.

The second thing was that he'd never been that social.

There were times he'd thought it would be good to meet another woman. You could do that down there. Nobody ever seemed to stay single all that long in his brother's park. But you had to go to the dinners and dances to do that, you had to have a certain spirit for the thing.

While he didn't even have the spirit to answer this goddamn door here.

He put on a robe and pair of slippers and shuffled

14

over. He'd forgotten to turn on the porch light again so he flicked it on now and opened the door.

"Vic."

Vic Manetti was standing in the yellow light. There was a trooper leaning on the squad car behind him but at that distance Peters couldn't make out who he was.

Manetti was "the new guy." Sheriff of Dead River for well over two years now but still "the new guy" to most people because he came from New York City and wasn't local.

"Sorry to wake you, George."

"That's all right."

Peters respected him. He'd pushed a few back with Manetti in the Caribou from time to time—and talking about what went on in town these days, sort of keeping in touch, Peters had the impression that he was a pretty good cop. He was calm, he had brains and he was thorough. You couldn't ask much more in a sawdust-and-cinders little burg like this.

But now, standing there, Peters thought he'd never seen the man so uncomfortable.

"I need to talk to you, George," he said.

"I guess you do. You want to come inside?"

"Actually I was hoping you'd be willing to come with us."

He watched the man shift around inside himself looking for the right thing to say. Then he guessed he found it.

"I need you to look at something for me. I need your expertise on something."

15

"Expertise?" He had to smile. It wasn't a word you heard much in Dead River.

"I got to warn you. It's ugly."

And Peters had a feeling then—maybe it was the word *expertise* clicking in—but some kind of light went off in his brain telling him that he knew what Manetti was talking about.

He managed to hope he was wrong.

"Give me a minute."

He walked back inside and took off the robe and slippers, found a shirt in the drawer neatly folded—neatness, even with the drinking, being something he knew Mary would have wanted him to hold on to—and a pair of shoes by the bed. He went to the kitchen. He opened the refrigerator and took out a carton of orange juice and gulped a couple of swallows. Then he went into the bathroom and splashed some water on his face and brushed his teeth. The face in the mirror looked all its sixty-six years and then some.

He walked back to the bedroom and took his wallet off the dresser. Her photo stood there smiling at him, an aging woman but still handsome. Way before the cancer.

Out of habit, distracted by the sight of her picture the way he guessed he almost always was, he opened the top drawer and had the .38 and its holster halfway out before he realized he wasn't going to need it this time.

He could leave the guns to the youngsters.

Vic was in the squad car waiting for him. The trooper he couldn't make out before turned out to be

Miles Harrison. He'd known Miles since he was just a kid. For a while he'd been their paperboy. For some reason he could never quite hit the porch. They'd cursed him every winter.

He said hello, asked after Miles' mom and dad, who were fine, thanks, and got in back. They started up. And then he was looking at the backs of their heads through the plate-glass-and-wire-mesh screen.

A funny place, he thought, for an old ex-sheriff to be riding.

Half an hour later the scotch was trying to slide up out of him and he was remembering his breathing, trying to keep it the hell down.

The kitchen was a goddamn slaughterhouse.

He stood there looking at what was left of the woman and the sitter and he knew right away what he had here. He'd known since seeing the urine sprayed across the stairs outside . . . that someone had *marked* the place.

And so, he guessed, did Manetti.

"You see why I wanted you," he said.

Peters nodded.

"The babysitter's mother called it in. Her name's Nancy Ann David, by the way, sixteen years old last March. The mother said it was getting late so she started phoning, but nobody answered. She tried some more until it got her worried and then she called us."

"The woman?"

He looked down at the body on the floor. Like the sitter on the table it was naked and both its arms and

17

legs were gone. There was a hole cut in the chest that somebody had pulled wide apart, breaking up the rib cage, and there was nothing in there where the heart was supposed to be. The skull was split and the brains were gone. Intestines trailed across the linoleum floor.

"Her name is Loreen Ellen Kaltsas. Thirty-six years old. Separated. Husband's name is Dean Allan Kaltsas. We've got him in custody and I talked to him down at the station. Evidently they didn't much care for each other. And he admits to smacking her around. But I don't think there's any connection. He seems pretty damn worried about the baby."

"The baby's how old, did you say?"

"Eighteen months. No sign of her anywhere. No blood on the crib, none in her room. Nothing."

He stepped around the blood and urine to the girl on the table. Max Joseph, the county coroner, was working on her.

"George."

"Hello, Max."

"How do you like this? Here we go again, huh?"

"Christ, Max, I hope not."

He made himself look at her. On this one most of the left breast was gone too, sliced away.

"Well I'll tell you, the reason I think we've got another go-round, George, is what's *not* here. All the meaty bits, if you catch my drift. Familiar?"

He didn't answer.

"Cause of death?"

"Hell, George, they ripped her heart out."

He looked down at the open blue eyes. Nancy Ann

18

David had been pretty once. Not what anyone would call a beauty, but pretty. He'd bet there were boyfriends out there. People who'd miss her.

"What about the woman?"

"Blow to the head. Probably an ax or a hatchet. Died instantly."

He walked back through the kitchen. Manetti was waiting in the dayroom. Together they walked outside. He needed some air.

Vic offered him a cigarette. He took it and they lit up. The sky was starting to brighten now, it had that nice early-morning glow, and you could hear the birds starting to replace the crickets.

"What do you think?" asked Manetti.

He heard the subtext. *You're the only one left who's been there. You're the only one who'd know for sure.*

Everyone else had either died that night or had moved away—to someplace they wouldn't have to think and remember so much every time they walked out into the woods or went for a swim by the shoreline.

He ought to have done the same.

But for Mary maybe he would have, but Mary had been born in Dead River and wanted to stay.

Still the nightmares should have been enough to tell him. *Go. Get out of here.* The nightmares and all that came to him unbidden practically every day until he lifted that second or third glass of scotch. Mostly the boy, naked, drifting toward him through his sights and Peters telling him to stop but him not stopping and the shotguns roaring, all opening up at once and . . .

19

And Mary was dead now. He had no family.

The town was strangers.

He should have gone.

He could still go.

Fuck the heat in Sarasota. They had air-conditioning, didn't they?

"Some kind of copycat, do you think?" Manetti's voice was trying to sound hopeful.

Peters looked at him. He looked tired, his thin, wiry body starting to curve into one big question mark. Manetti wasn't so young anymore either.

"After eleven years, Vic? A copycat? After eleven years go by?"

He threw down the cigarette. The stink of flesh and blood was still there in his nostrils. The cigarette couldn't compete.

That and the other stink.

The one he remembered like a stab wound somewhere that had never healed—that would probably never heal.

The woman, bleeding, hurling herself down the cliffside, her knife slashing Daniels ear to ear. . . .

"What I think," he said.

He stepped on the cigarette guttering in the grass and looked out across the hills, gray but visible now, leading down through the forest to the cliffs and to the sea. Not so far away.

He listened for the birds. A good clean morning sound, dependable and real as daylight. The bird sounds helped.

"What I think," he said, "is that we missed some last time. And I think they've been away for a little while."

4:47 A.M.

By the time David Halbard looked up from his Mac it was dawn. *Enough,* he thought, though he felt no strain.

He pushed away from his desk in the leather swivel chair, released the floppy disks from their disk drives, and filed them.

The night had gone by fast and well. Ever since college he'd been able to do this—pull all-nighters—if there was sufficient challenge to the project.

College was thirteen years ago. He had the thinning hair to prove it. But his energy hadn't diminished. Just keep the coffee coming and he was fine.

David Halbard was a satisfied man. He was right now. Sipping the dregs of his tired fifth cup.

He was always a bit surprised to find himself feeling that way. His first year out of the University of Pennsylvania via Brooklyn Polytechnic had been a disaster after all. Engineering school had prepared

21

him for the big design work, but the job at Comcorp had turned out to be completely by the book, nothing even remotely sexy. He gave it a year and a half and then quit, trusting to luck.

The job at IBM was better—a big new machine for the U.S. Coast Guard. He and two other guys had done most of the work themselves and they'd had a terrific time. But halfway through, the Guard had scrapped the project. Too complex, they said.

It wasn't too complex as far as the team was concerned. It was just that the Guard was so fucking simple.

The next three years saw two more designs come and go, and by 1986 he'd had it. Total burnout, total discouragement. At this rate he was going to wind up designing transformers somewhere or something equally boring, plugging away all day and hating himself, and hating Amy for putting up with him.

By then he'd married her, his former assistant at IBM—similarly, her job was way beneath her—the single grace note in his messy, discordant life. They decided to simplify, to pick a place they liked and find some way to make it work. They had a little savings. They'd repair TVs and radios if they had to.

They were young and smart and what the hell.

The place was easy to come by. Amy came from Portland originally and still thought of Maine as home. And David, Brooklyn born, thought the coast of Maine looked fine.

He still did.

He turned off the Mac, got out of his chair and

walked to the double plate-glass doors to the sun deck. He slid one open to let in the morning air.

There was a breeze ruffling the tall grass and goldenrod beyond the stand of oaks but the day was going to be mild.

Small birds fluttered through the branches, assembling, singing in the trees.

One more cup, he thought, *out here on the deck.*

He walked through the study back to the kitchen and poured himself a mugful.

Coffee never kept him awake. Work did.

Work was supposed to.

He took the mug outside and sat in one of the green wooden lawn chairs along the weathered railing.

Over his head two thick branches swayed in the breeze. The largest branch reached all the way across the deck, nearly fingering the bedroom window adjacent to the study.

Amy lay sleeping inside.

Got to cut that back one of these days, he thought.

But he didn't like to touch them, really. There were ten trees, spaced unevenly, all black oak, tall and old and venerable, and they seemed to deserve their living space.

It was unusual for trees to grow as big as these this far north. The cold winter winds off the sea kept most things stunted, hunched low to the ground. Humbled.

He wiggled his toes and sipped his coffee.

He was barefoot. The sun had warmed the deck already.

23

The deck was painted pinewood, gray, and it was roomy, twelve by thirty-five, room enough for four comfortable chairs, a picnic table with benches and a grill. Stilts pegged it to the side of a steep hill that rolled down through the stand of oak and scrub and flattened out to over three full acres of grasslands, another two acres of low pine, fir and cedar, and beyond that, to the point—to the cliffs and the sea.

You couldn't see the cliffs through the pines. But the view was still spectacular in its way. Nothing trimmed. Nothing mowed or planted. Everything wild.

The woods are dark, he thought.

Thank god for that.

It was the game that had bought them the place.

Two years before, while he was still writing code into ROM and then debugging, while Amy was designing the graphics and Phil was composing the music back in New York, they'd rented. A hundred-year-old house back in the woods. Charming except when it rained, because then the roof leaked in about a dozen places. You had a symphony of pots and pans. And nothing left to cook with at all.

But his idea for a fast, tense, really *scary* horror-adventure game turned out to be right on the money. Computer Arts had snapped it up, licensing American rights at a royalty rate that struck him as surprisingly generous. And "The Woods Are Dark" became their first big win against Nintendo. In fact it was *anybody's* first big win against Nintendo—they'd dominated the market for so long.

Part of the reason was the controversy. His design had included hordes of spiders coming to devour you through trembling sticky webs, writhing snake pits, deformed half-human monsters popping out of trees, from behind bushes, and a graveyard where the dead hauled themselves slowly, painfully, hand over hand out of their graves. What you killed, bled. Bled plenty.

Amy's graphics were state of the art and shivery as hell and people were offended that it was mostly kids who would be playing with this thing.

But neither David nor Computer Arts saw it that way. Compared to a PG-rated movie these days the game was innocent as Scrabble.

Compared to every other game it was a stick of dynamite.

So sales went through the roof, allowing the company to buy more games, all of which were selling, too.

But "The Woods Are Dark" was Computer Arts' equivalent to Nintendo's "Super Mario Brothers." No other game had topped it either here or in Japan—it was raking in as much over there now as it was at home. And the advance for the new game, "Hide and Seek," was stunning.

So he and Amy went house shopping.

What they found was this, a gray cedar-shake salt-box with a view—also about a hundred years old and as isolated as the rental had been, with their nearest neighbor almost two miles north, but light-years from the other house in terms of upkeep. It had been owned by an old country doctor and his wife until he died and she moved to Arizona to be with her children. They'd had enough money and stubborn Yankee respect for things past to keep the house pretty much what it had been originally, to keep the hand-hewn beams exposed and the moldings stained, not painted, and to hold on to the old potbellied stove.

Next week Campbell and his crew were bolting the sills to the foundation for the new addition. Much of the lumber was already piled under the deck, covered by tarps. He'd seen Campbell's work and knew the man to be a meticulous craftsman, one who could be counted upon to keep the feel of the place and blend the old skillfully with the new. He was expensive but well worth the price.

And hell, they had the money. Miraculously, they had a lot more money than either of them knew what to do with.

His brokers knew.

Nintendo had one thing right, he thought. Roughly translated from the Japanese, the word *nintendo* meant, "no matter how hard you work, the results are in the hands of god."

He figured that said it all.

The coffee was almost gone.

The sun was warming. He was starting to feel drowsy. He heard the sudden whir of wings and saw a bird beat hard out of the tall grass. Grouse, partridge, pheasant—some kind of game bird—he wished he knew more about these things. The bird flew a hundred yards or so and settled back into the grass again. He watched until it disappeared.

Then looked back to where it had come from.

And damn near dropped his coffee.

It was far away but his eyes were pretty good, and

OFFSPRING

even if they'd only been half as good there was no mistaking what was out there.

She was standing in the grass and goldenrod. The grass was maybe three feet high, just up to her waist. If he had to guess, he'd say she was seventeen or eighteen. A teenager.

He couldn't make out her features but her hair was dark and long, very long. Covering her naked shoulders. Half hiding her breasts.

He couldn't say about the rest of her, but from the waist on up she was naked.

Holding a flower and turning it in her hands. A red one.

She was looking in his direction.

At the house, or at him.

Amy's not going to believe this, he thought. *Our very own wood sprite out here in the yard.*

The girl stood a moment longer and then turned and walked toward the pines, a wild thick cascade of dark brown hair disappearing slowly through the bright yellow grass.

He had to wake Amy and tell her.

He walked back into the study and slid the door closed behind him. He was on his way to their bedroom, passing the old Defiant potbellied stove in the middle of the study when he glanced at the clock.

Five-thirty.

She'll kill me, he thought.

With good reason. Amy hadn't been sleeping well in the past three months since Melissa was born, though Melissa was evolving (with incredible rapidity, he

27

thought—it was amazing how swiftly infants changed) into a good easy baby who didn't tend to wake them every half hour like some of the others he'd known. He'd only had to tend to her once tonight.

And Amy'd slept through it soundly for a change.

Let her go, he thought. The news could keep.

He peeked in on his way to the bathroom.

Her body had come back fast and he was pleased to see her sleeping naked again, the strong back, the slope of shoulder and the curve of her breast pressed into the bedsheet.

On the other side of the room Melissa lay tiny and pink faced in her bassinet.

You're a pretty lucky sonovabitch, he thought. *You know that?*

Home and wife and baby.

Wood nymph and all.

Out in the field he heard the first crow of the morning.

5:02 A.M.

Second Stolen moved through the shadows of the pine and cedar forest, breathing deeply of its sweet smell. Beneath her feet the fallen needles were thick, cool, wet with dew. A low branch brushed her thigh and made her nipples stiffen.

Sensation entered her more deeply than it did the others. She was not exactly pleased by this, but she knew it to be true.

She was nearing the edge of the forest. Already she could hear the sea.

She had not yet found the children. But it was dawn now. She had to return.

The Woman would be angry.

The Woman had sensed something. The Woman had sent Second Stolen to find the children—and she had not.

She felt a sullen shame.

She was not the hunter the Woman wished her to be.

29

At the end she had drifted to the house where the infant was, thinking dimly of her own child, who was hardly any older. But it was early and the infant had not appeared yet. Only the man, who had seen her.

She wondered if it mattered that the man had seen her.

There was only one way to cool the Woman's anger, and that was to anticipate it. As she walked she watched for the proper instrument.

It needed to be thin and strong and supple.

There.

The branch was green, tough, but her hands were calloused hard and she twisted it to the right, down and then up, splitting through the filaments of sapwood. She peeled away the needles. The wood bled in her hand.

She walked to the clearing, squinting at the sun.

Fat black bumblebees drifted through the hawkweed, daisies, and clover. She stood among them, knowing the bees were harmless unless you hit or stepped on one. The bees flew low around her, gathering pollen on their long black legs.

Apart from the bees she was alone.

Across the clearing the surf pounded.

She brought the branch down across her back, striking hard, knowing that each blow must mark her or else there was no sense to it. She used it across her buttocks and thighs but did not dare to strike lower than that. She did not wish to stir the bees.

Sensation entered her more deeply than it did the others.

When she was finished her hand was black with bark and sap.

Beyond the field the woods grew thick again. The path twisted up and then down through a long shaded canopy of gnarled scrubby pitch pine and spruces, beaten low by the offshore winds.

She walked through them to the cliffs, found the path again and started down.

Halfway down she saw them, all six of them below her scrambling over the rocks at the shoreline. The Girl carried a bag. The others did not go empty handed either though it was too far away to see what they had gathered.

It was dawn and they were moving quickly, silently.

They would be there long before her.

The Woman would be angry.

She could call to them. Make them wait. The Woman might not question her, might think she had found them after all. Though it had taken her nearly all night and into the morning.

Except that she was marked already.

She was naked, and the Woman would read the marks and know.

On the trail before her lay a fox scat. She used the stick to pick it apart and saw the matted hair and bone—the fox's meal of mouse or rabbit.

Its prey had known pain before it died. Had struggled against it.

She sighed at what could not be helped and continued on alone.

7:20 A.M.

The map was out.

It wasn't the same map they'd used eleven years ago but it might as well have been—it was that crinkled up and beat to hell—and it hung against the same old smoke-stained slate gray station-house wall.

The last time Peters had seen the place was at his retirement party.

Mary had been there, looking pretty and openly relieved that he was finally getting out. A few of the other wives were there, those who knew him well and still cared to know him, and when they presented him with the pair of welded, four-inch-thick solid brass balls, some of the wives had blushed.

The time before that was the time he'd made his last arrest.

He was clearing out his desk when this skinny little weasel of a kid walks in to post his buddy's bail. The buddy'd been picked up for drunken driving and reckless endangerment and he'd been there two, three days or so. They'd set bail at $1,200.

So this kid is fishing through his pockets for the money, sort of fumbling around in there. He's nervous and Peters is watching him, wondering why. And then he *sees* why, because when the kid pulls out the cash, out pops a plastic baggie. The kid makes a grab for it but it falls to the floor.

Peters walks over and picks it up.

What's this? he says to the kid.

There's about a half an ounce of Thai stick there.

Aw hell, says the kid. Ah dammit. Ah shit.

Peters read him his rights right then and there. And as soon as they had him in the holding cell Peters accepted the bail money for his friend. Gave him a receipt for the amount. Unfortunately $1,200 was all the kid had on him. So that once that was gone he couldn't make the measly $150 for his own bail. Peters had often wondered how long the buddy'd let him stew there.

He'd meant to ask Manetti but he kept forgetting.

Manetti and Miles Harrison were listening now. Peters was pointing at the map.

"We didn't know what we had eleven years ago," he said. "Or where to find it. This time I think you can assume we do. Let's say they roam afield a bit, which means they could be anywhere along the coast from here to Lubec and maybe down to Cutler. There's plenty of forest all through this area and we can't afford to rule that out but I'd bet on the actual shoreline, on one of the caves in here. That's where we found them last time.

"It's still a hell of a job. This whole damn area's honeycombed with caves. But last time it was night already when we got started. One in the morning. We couldn't help that. But here we got some daylight hours to use so I suggest you move as fast as you can. Call in everybody you've got including the State Highway boys and do it *yesterday*."

Manetti looked at Harrison. The younger man didn't need to be told.

"I'll handle it," he said. He walked over to the next cubicle and they could hear him on the phone in there.

Manetti was looking at the map. Worried. Running his hand over his face and through his curly hair.

"You know what I don't get?" he said. "Where the hell could they have *been so* long? How come nobody's seen them? I mean, you do this kind of thing, you get noticed. So where've they been hiding?"

It was seven in the morning but Peters could still have used a drink. Time was as fluid as the booze was. It all depended on what was going on inside.

"I'll tell you, Vic," he said, "I thought about that. I don't think they *were* hiding. I think that what they were doing was moving."

"Moving?"

"Look. We're a spit in the eye from Canada here. Plenty of coastline all along the gulf, all the way up to Newfoundland. Maybe even up into Hudson Bay. Plenty of places to wander. Some of it practically deserted. We don't tend to coordinate missing persons stats too terrifically with Canada, at least I know we didn't in my day. And I assume that hasn't changed.

35

But I bet if we asked they've had some funny ones over the years along that coast."

"We'll check it out," Manetti said.

"When we're finished here," said Peters. "When we've got 'em. When it's just mop-up."

He reflected that he'd been saying we again all morning. He hoped it wasn't getting in Manetti's way that he seemed to be finding himself playing top cop again.

Then again, if it was, there wasn't a whole lot he could do about it except try to watch his language. They'd asked him in. So there he was.

"You know what?" he said. "I bet they don't even know they crossed a border. I bet it never even occurred to them. I bet they just kept moving."

Unless you were looking at maps, he thought, borders were fluid too.

Manetti nodded.

"So where do you want to start?" he said.

And for a moment Peters saw Caggiano again—his neck torn open, trying to scream. Manetti looked a little like him, actually. Wiry.

He dumped the memory.

"We find that cave," he said. "We find the cave and hope they're calling it home again."

PART II

AFTERNOON

11:00 A.M.

Amy was just getting around to the breakfast dishes when she heard him turn on the shower in the bathroom. She wondered how much sleep he'd gotten and felt a familiar envy. David could get by on five or six hours a night, no problem. Whereas she needed eight and suffered when she didn't get them.

Which had been most of the time, since Melissa was born.

This third month, though, was easier. Melissa's patterns of sleeping, eating and alertness were becoming much more regular. She was sleeping as much as nine or ten hours a night now, waking only once or twice.

Her *own* sleeping patterns were the problem now. She hadn't yet adjusted. Last night had been her first really sound night's sleep in weeks.

It felt good. But it was hardly enough.

41

Whereas David liked to quote Warren Zevon—"I'll sleep when I'm dead."

She didn't know where he got his energy. Not from his parents, that was for sure. His parents' idea of an evening had been three or four sitcoms, news at eleven, and bed.

It was one of the few things she didn't understand about him and it didn't amount to much. Otherwise, their minds worked similarly in most of the ways that counted. And they talked.

It was pretty much all you needed.

She stacked the last of the dishes in the dishwasher and dried her hands. Her skin was getting dry again and she made a mental note to cream them. Having no fingernails that were longer than a sixteenth of an inch was bad enough—Keyboard Nails Syndrome practically came with the territory—but she didn't need flaky skin as well.

Hormonally speaking there'd been a few changes since the delivery. On the upside, it had finally stabilized her wildly irregular period. On the downside, she couldn't even drink so much as a single glass of white wine anymore without risking losing her supper—though vodka sat fine for some reason.

That, and her hands got dry.

It wasn't too bad as trade-offs went.

Especially when you factored in Melissa.

She was napping and Amy was loath to wake her. But now that David was up she needed to get to the vacuuming. Claire and Luke were expected around two and she wanted to get in at least an hour's work on the design before they arrived.

So she supposed she'd have to risk it.

Nah, she thought. *Get to work now. Let David do the vacuuming after he's had breakfast.*

He won't mind. He never did.

Her PC was directly across the big oak desk from his. Sitting there together facing one another on those—nowadays—rare times that their schedules coincided they'd kid about feeling like the Fabulous Baker Boys, sans Michelle Pfeiffer. David sans hairpiece.

She poured a cup of coffee, dosed it with milk from the Coolerator, went to the desk and sat down.

She used her toe to switch on the power tap and pushed her disks into the disk drive. Then sat back ready to look at yesterday's work.

While it booted up she thought of Claire.

She should have been happy thinking about Claire, but the way things were these days the first feeling that came was anger. Not at her—she and Claire had been best friends since college, and nothing had changed about that.

But at Steven, her husband.

She'd seen it from the first, almost ten years ago.

Unfortunately, Claire hadn't.

Something vaguely *sneaky* about him. A kind of spinelessness behind all the good humor and courtesy and all his supposed caring for Claire. He had the habit of indirection, of never quite looking at you when he was talking to you. Then you'd catch him staring at you when you'd been looking elsewhere.

The men all liked him. Even David. *Mister Regular Guy.* Always ready with a drink or a laugh.

Amy hadn't trusted him for a minute.

She'd told Claire as much, as gently but firmly as she could, as soon as she realized that they were heading for marriage.

But he'd been smart. The way these low-level sociopath types were often smart, she guessed. He'd played it perfectly. He'd come on like a friend and nothing more for months before declaring himself a potential lover. Got her into the habit of being around him—after a while, pretty much constantly. Edging into her circle of friends. Nice and easy.

Claire was on the rebound at the time. She'd finally found the strength to dump the guy she'd been living with since college, a guy so jealous and possessive and so *inappropriate* in his jealousy it would have been comical had it not led to a series of raging arguments, which culminated in a drunken scene one night outside her apartment with the boy proclaiming loudly that she was no goddamn better than his mother. By then Claire was vulnerable to the soft approach. And Steven had it down pat.

We'll be friends first and foremost, he always seemed to say. *I respect you.*

Amy remembered it well, cloying and phony.

But coming off this other maniac it was perfect. The sex was good. And it was easy for Claire to mistake attentiveness for caring. To assume he actually *liked* her. Loved her.

Amy doubted that Steven had ever liked or loved anybody.

She often wondered when, and why, Steven had decided he wanted her. Claire was uncommonly pretty and maybe that was it, because Steven was headed for some high-powered New York law firm, everybody who knew him was aware of that, and Claire would look good on his arm, good to the partners and to the clients, and because she was modest and graceful, even good to their wives.

She'd warned her. Probably too often. But Claire hadn't bought her arguments—either then, about the marriage, or later, about the advisability of having children by him.

Luke.

Poor Luke.

With a forger for a father.

When she thought about that and thought about Claire these days she felt angry and sad and wished to god she had the power to hurt the bastard.

And lucky. She also felt lucky.

She could hear David running water in the sink. He always wasted water when he shaved but if that was all the trouble you had with a guy—that and the fact that he could never remember to put the toilet seat down and dropped his goddamn ashes all over the place because he could never seem to find an ashtray when he needed one—you didn't have trouble at all. And you damn well knew it.

Her father, bless him, had told her she would meet a man like this one day and she had never believed him, perhaps because part of her thought her father *was* that man and she'd come across nobody even vaguely like him. Yet one day there he was. Sexy, thoughtful, a good partner and by now, a proven good companion. He shared the chores, the responsibilities with Melissa, diapered her, fed her, got up nights those first two difficult months . . . and clearly saw in Amy an equal both at work and in their marriage.

She had come to recognize a certain distance in him since his father had died of cancer three years ago. He had loved the lazy, sweet old man and he'd taken it hard. She knew he brooded on it occasionally. When she questioned him he'd only say he missed him. The words rang true. But she wondered if, without him knowing it, his feelings also ran deeper.

He worked so long, so late and hard. As though racing some internal clock. Lately he'd talked about quitting smoking.

She wondered if he was starting to become afraid of death. If his father's dying had added some ambiguous, questionable rider to the document of his own mortality.

I'll sleep when I'm dead.

If so, he didn't seem aware of it.

And he certainly didn't look aware of anything remotely like that now, walking into the study in his washed-out red terry bathrobe and unlaced tennis sneakers. He looked alive and fresh and just a little ridiculous.

"Got a start on the third board last night," he said. He leaned over and kissed the top of her head, nuzzled her long curly red hair. She smelled soap and papaya shampoo.

She was grateful that he was a man who had no truck with aftershave.

"I know. I looked it over first thing this morning. You got a lot done. Looks good."

"Thank you."

"You're very welcome."

"Coffee?"

"On the stove."

"Terrific."

From the kitchen he said, "What time's Claire coming?"

"Twoish."

"Good. Gives me time to fix the cord on the table lamp. Shorted out on me last night, around two in the morning. I've got to reinsulate the wire. We've got electrician's tape floating around here somewhere, don't we?"

"There's some in the basement, I think."

He walked back into the study and looked over her shoulder at the monitor. Then he looked down at her breasts where the robe had fallen away.

"How are you making out?"

"I haven't really started. I got to thinking about Claire."

He nodded, sipped his coffee. They'd discussed it all before. She didn't need to explain. She knew he felt pretty much the same. He was Claire's friend too.

"Listen," she said. "How'd you like to run the vacuum in about an hour? Let Melissa sleep till then. So that I can do some work here."

"No problem."

He walked to the glass double doors. The sun was bright outside. He opened them and a breeze ruffled the papers beside her.

"Jesus!" he said. "I almost forgot. An *amazing* thing this morning! Are we aware of some retro-hip latter-day commune out this way? Something on that order?"

47

She looked up from the monitor.

"Excuse me?"

"There was a girl out here this morning, way on out in the field. A little after dawn. Real long hair and naked as my mother bore me."

"A girl?"

"Yeah. Sixteen, seventeen maybe. She was pretty far away."

"Naked?"

"From the waist up, anyway. I couldn't see the rest."

"You're kidding."

"Unh-unh."

"Nice breasts?"

"As I said, she was pretty far away."

"Hmmm."

She got up from the monitor and walked over to him. She put her arms around his waist.

"You didn't invite her in?"

"Why should I? Who wants the wood nymph when you got the goddess?"

She laughed. "Pretty saggy goddess."

"Goddesses don't sag. They ripen. As do the wheat and the corn."

"Corn is just about right."

She kissed him. He smelled of soap and coffee. His mouth was smooth.

"I'm not going to get much work done, am I?" she said.

"Not at the moment. And I'm not going to get to insulate the wire."

"Let's not wake Melissa."

48

"Don't worry, I'm not planning on running the Electrolux either."

He opened her robe, pushed it off her shoulders and lowered her on top of him to the couch, and the sun was warm on her back as she drew him up inside her.

She remembered that the monitor was still on, her program running.

It was the last thought she had for a while that wasn't strictly for the two of them.

11:50 A.M.

Peters stood in the mouth of the cave, sweating. It wasn't just the climb. It was nerves.

Behind him Manetti, Harrison, and the four state troopers were jittery too. You could see it in the beams of their flashlights scudding across the fire-blackened walls.

Even if you didn't know what happened here the place was unnerving.

He shouldered the shotgun, knowing already he wasn't going to be needing it, and stepped inside.

Remembering what it was like.

The man, Nicholas something, the name strangely lost to him now, wearing glasses that flew off his face as they opened fire, mistaking him for one of them despite the glasses, they were so damn scared, killing him after all he'd been through, after he and the woman on the floor, naked, bleeding, torn to hell but still alive, had done most of their

51

killing for them. He remembered shooting the one with the knife.

And then he remembered the boy . . .

. . . who'd been their captive god only knew how long, walking toward them, his arms held out in front of him, walking in that slow dreamy glide, so filthy and caked with his own dried blood that it was easy to figure he was one of them too, and when Peters told him to stop and he didn't stop they were taking no chances by then and all six shotguns opened up at once, and whether Peters had killed him or somebody else had killed him Peters would never know.

That was eleven years ago and he was glad he'd stopped for the pint of Johnny Walker. He was glad he wasn't a cop anymore, that he could pull the pint out of his pocket and break the seal and unscrew it and tilt it back and drink deep. Like he was doing now.

The others were watching. Rookie troopers cradling newer shotguns, disapproving.

Fuck 'em.

He was glad he wasn't a cop for lots of reasons.

But especially the boy.

He needed not to think about the boy.

He drank again and pocketed the bottle and looked around.

It was gone now—the skins, the rags, the clothing. They'd taken it all to the beach, right down to the last broken ax handle, the last gun stock, rake and leather belt, and burned it two days later. What didn't burn and what they didn't need to bag for identification they took to the old town dump on Tucker Road where most of it had come from in the first place.

Now all he saw here were a few bent nails and a tarnished doorknob on the hard dirt floor and that was that.

They hadn't been back. Not to this place.

Who knew? Maybe they had memories too.

"Shit," said Manetti.

They were all, in their way, disappointed. Relieved, sure. But disappointed. It had been so easy for him to find this place again even after eleven years without so much as passing it by in all that time that Peters guessed they figured they were getting lucky. And now they weren't lucky. They were like dogs who'd lost the scent.

"There's a smaller room off to the rear there. Might check it."

He leveled the shotgun in front of him again. But it was training, mostly. It was habit. They weren't here and they hadn't been. The cave smelled of earth and damp and seawater. If they'd stayed any time at all it would have smelled . . . otherwise.

Manetti found the broken pitchfork tine way back in a corner.

Apart from that, nothing.

Peters felt himself sag, his body go slack. He took a pull on the whiskey.

They walked out the way they came in.

Nobody said anything for a while. They started down the mountain.

The sea breeze felt good blowing through his hair. Good and clean.

Midway down he asked Manetti about the dogs

and Manetti said they'd be in from Bangor by two o'clock along with another twenty troopers.

As of now they had two more parties of six men each working a narrow range north and south along the coastline. The troopers and the dogs would take the woods when they arrived, spread farther north to Lubec and farther south to Cutler, and some of the dogs would work the scent off the Kaltsas place.

Two o'clock gave them four more hours of daylight. Four hours.

He stepped down off the path.

It was exactly here that he had put the pump to the woman's eye so there was no possibility of missing and pulled the trigger. It was already too late for Caggiano. Her jaws were still in his neck when they pulled her off him.

Manetti saw him pause.

"Everything okay, George?" he said.

Peters nodded.

"Look, you found the cave. You told us where else you think they're likely to be and what you think they're likely to do. I don't see that there's any more reason for me to put you through this. Maybe you should go home and get some sleep and let us go from here."

Peters shook his head. "I know 'em," he said. "I shot them all to hell that day and I saw what they had in there and I questioned the survivor. You need me. I know what you're thinking and it's kind of you. But you'd do a whole lot better to ask me nicely to please stick around."

Manetti smiled. "Hey. Stick around, will you, George?"

"Sure. Sure I will."

He stopped in the sand a moment and stared up the rock face.

From where he stood it was almost impossible to see the entrance. They'd chosen it well. He wondered how they'd done choosing the new one.

And thinking that he must have looked sort of pained because Manetti said, "How was it? Pretty rough walking back in there?"

"I've had better memories," he said. "Better days."

He reached for the pint in his pocket again and unscrewed the cap. He said, "But it'll get rougher, Vic. You're going to want to join me before it's through. Hell, you probably will join me."

And drank from the bottle.

2:20 P.M.

Amy looked at Claire across the kitchen table and knew she'd done the right thing inviting her.

"You look tired," she said. "You getting any sleep at all?"

"Not enough. Not lately."

She reached for Melissa's tiny hand. The hand immediately gripped her index finger. She never stopped nursing for a second. "She's so *beautiful*," Claire said.

Amy's breast was getting sore. She'd need to switch over in a minute or two. But she smiled. Claire was right. Melissa *was* beautiful. Soft pink skin, a dusting of fine brown hair. And the prettiest big brown eyes. She even *smelled* beautiful—all sweet breath and warm clean skin.

Melissa had been sleeping when they arrived. Claire and Luke had tiptoed into the bedroom and Claire said afterward that it was love at first sight.

Even Luke was beaming—as if it were his own baby sister he was staring at.

Claire withdrew her finger. The baby clutched Amy's breast instead.

"They're serving him the papers today," Claire said.

"It's about time."

"It took them till Monday just to find him. Turns out he was back with Marion again, back in the office. Working off the books. As legal consultant or something. Not a partner again, god knows, but back."

"Marion. *That* bitch."

"I don't know why, but for some reason she seems to be willing to do just about anything for him."

"You want to bet she's screwing him?"

"I don't know. I never thought Marion was the type to get involved with a partner. I thought she was just your basic shark. But get this, though. It was Marion's *secretary* who notarized the loan."

"Ow!" It was Amy's nipple that hurt, not the information.

Claire flinched. Amy almost laughed. It was as though it were Claire's breast and not Amy's that the tiny jaws had pinched.

She shifted Melissa to the other breast. Melissa didn't cry. Miraculously, she almost never cried now.

Claire smiled, looking relieved, as the baby nuzzled in.

It struck her as a little strange. She'd nursed Luke, hadn't she? Of course she had. She remembered it clearly. So why the squeamishness over a little bite?

She let it pass.

"Wait a minute," she said. "I want to get this right.

Marion's secretary notarized the loan to cover his debt to the firm, correct?"

"Uh-huh."

"So she knew all about the forgery. They both did."

"She had to."

"Absolutely unbelievable."

Unbeknownst to Claire, Steven had taken out a loan nine months ago, about a year into their separation, for well over a half million dollars—Amy couldn't remember the figure exactly. The loan was to cover half the out-of-court settlement of a former client's suit against the firm. The firm was absorbing the other half.

Steven had somehow mismanaged the client's funds. It wasn't the first time he'd been accused of that and this time the firm was holding him accountable.

So he put up their home in Greenwich as collateral. And forged Claire's signature to the documents.

Half a million was the entire value of their house, less the mortgage.

At the time, with Steven's support as erratic as it was, Claire and Luke were just barely getting by.

Then he got himself fired, lost his partnership over some new problem. Nobody knew what, and nobody at the firm was telling.

They just called in his loan.

First the support dried up. Then Steven disappeared completely.

He'd given up his lease on the apartment in Manhattan and left no forwarding address. Neither Claire nor Luke had seen or heard from him in over six months. Christmas and Luke's birthday had come and gone without a word from him.

59

Her job as a secretary didn't even cover the mortgage payments, never mind food and clothing.

And now his creditors were howling. Howling to Claire.

Hell, they couldn't *find* Steven.

And the loan wasn't his only forgery, either. He'd signed her name to their tax return last year so she wouldn't know they were into the IRS for over a quarter of a million dollars.

So the IRS was howling too.

They didn't care who signed the goddamn papers. It was a joint return and they wanted the money.

God only knew what else was out there. Waiting to pounce.

In a few months' time she'd gone from pretty well off to flat broke, with no credit and in debt to the neck. The half-million-dollar loan, the mortgage, gas and electric, credit cards, car payments—all were with collection agencies by now.

She didn't even answer the phone anymore; there were so many dunning calls. She spent cash she didn't have on a phone machine to screen them.

Amy and David had loaned her the money for a lawyer. The lawyer was trying to track Steven down to serve him papers for the divorce hearing—he'd done that now, finally—and work out reduction of liability deals with all parties concerned, based upon the forgeries. But even so she was going to lose the house. Pretty much all of it. If she was lucky she'd come out of it with thirty thousand dollars, the lawyer said.

She was thirty-seven. Luke was eight. They had

OFFSPRING

maybe thirty thousand to build a whole new life for themselves. It wasn't much.

Amy could feel her hurt. And her fear.

It crawled across the table to her like a spider and slid across her spine.

She hadn't seen Claire in two months now. Eight weeks. It was not much time. But the effects of strain had articulated themselves rapidly. The fine skin beneath the wide brown eyes looked bruised from lack of sleep. There were strands of silver in the long dark hair. Claire's body had always been lean and tight, even after Luke. Now it seemed to sag somehow, forced in upon itself. As though holding for too long a time a single, shallow breath.

She wished she could just hug her, hold her and tell her everything would be all right, that everything would be fine—even though it wasn't going to be all right, it was going to be a long rough haul and there was no use making believe otherwise.

She did the next best thing. She handed her Melissa across the table.

"Here. Hold her for a while. I'll get us some more coffee."

Melissa smiled, swiping with her hands, staring up at Claire delightedly, her eyes getting bigger and bigger.

Claire smiled too, brightening.

"Melissa!" she said, and started making the sounds people make when they're holding a baby. Melissa cooed right back at her.

There's nothing like three months' worth of baby for turning you around, she thought.

61

Unless, of course, it's four in the morning.

Stop bitching, she thought. *Things are so much better now.*

She returned with the coffee.

"Is Luke going to be all right out there?" Claire asked.

"Sure. David'll keep an eye on him. Besides, there's nothing much to get into except grass and bugs and trees."

"You're by the sea, aren't you?"

"Half a mile away. You figure he'll go that far?"

"I doubt it. He doesn't know much about the country."

"We'll take him down later if you want, show you both all the sights. The cliffs down at the point are pretty spectacular."

"Those I don't want him anywhere near."

"Once he sees them I think I can guarantee he'll be careful."

The phone rang. Amy got up and answered it.

Melissa was holding on to Claire's finger again, cooing happily.

Amy listened to the voice on the phone, too amazed to say anything, though there were a thousand things to say.

The voice went on for what seemed like a very long while. "Wait a minute," she said.

And when she came back to the table it was hard to keep the fury off her face. For Claire's sake, she tried.

How dare he? she thought.

She reached for her baby.

"It's for you," she said.

Claire looked puzzled.

"It's him," she said. "It's Steven. He says he's coming up here. He says he's on his way."

2:43 P.M.

The day was turning hot and slightly humid for this time of year.

David was with Will Campbell under the deck, the tarps pulled back so that Campbell could inspect the lumber.

Luke was there. He'd asked David's permission to go through his toolbox. Most of the tools had once belonged to David's father—which meant that they were basically unused—but David saw no harm in letting the boy root around in there. Through the open door to the shop he could watch Luke pulling out layers of sandpaper and packages of nails and screws to get at the hammers, rasps and screwdrivers underneath. He knew Luke was listening, interested for some reason in what they had to say, though he doubted the boy could understand very much of it.

They were standing by a pile of twelve-foot-long two-by-sixes tinted green, southern yellow pine that they'd use for the bottom layer, heavily treated against damp rot and insects. Planning the attack on the addition.

Will Campbell was a thin rangy man of about fifty, his face so deeply lined and tanned that to David he always seemed to be frowning.

He stamped out the butt of his Pall Mall. His hand moved gracefully over the board he was sighting.

"Pretty good," he said.

That coming from Campbell was high praise. David knew next to nothing about lumber but he was glad to hear it.

"But we gotta get 'em down fast," Campbell said. "A day in the sun and they'll warp like swizzle sticks. They'll do the trick, though. Now these . . ."

He stepped over to a much larger pile about four and a half feet high by four feet wide, a mix of spruce and balsam. Two-by-tens mostly, ranging from eight to twenty feet long. This was the framing lumber, the underpinnings for what was going to be the first-story flooring.

". . . these are *fine*," he said.

"Fine?" He smiled. He'd never heard Campbell use the word.

"Good local stuff right out of the Big Woods. Hardly any reaction wood at all that I can see. Good and regular."

"What's the Big Woods?" asked Luke. He stood in the door of the shop, a claw hammer in his hand that was much too heavy for him, pounding awkwardly at invisible nails.

"You're in it, son, sort of," said Campbell. "Scrappy

little part of it of course, way out here on the coast. But from Bangor on up's all Big Woods territory. Old growth. Logging country. Red spruce, black spruce, white spruce, cedar. Rivers, lakes, streams. You can pull trout out of the streams and you can flush a bear or a moose if you're of a mind to."

"You can?"

"Sometimes."

"I want to see a bear!" Luke took a wider swing, hammering a bear skull.

Campbell laughed. "In the wild? No you don't."

"Yes I do."

"A bear can move fast as an automobile over short distances and start up even faster. Think you can outrun a car, son?"

Luke frowned and thought about it. "Well, maybe if I was standing kind of far away I'd like to see one. Like through binoculars."

"Maybe then," said Campbell. "Sure. Why not?"

"Look over on the first shelf there," said David. "Right behind you."

Luke walked into the shop. The shelf, David knew, was just about reachable for him. He was tall for his age, with long thin arms like his mother's. They watched him look around and find them. He started to reach up and then caught himself, stopped and turned.

"Can I?" he asked.

"Sure you can," said David.

The binoculars were his father's too, old and not particularly high-powered, but in working order.

Luke looped the thong around his neck, dropped

the claw hammer noisily into the toolbox and looked
through the lenses.

"Know how to focus?" said David.

Luke shook his head. David walked over and
showed him.

"See, you've got two images here. Now you break
the lenses either toward your nose or away from your
nose until you've got just the one image," he said.
"Only one. Then you turn this knob until whatever
you want to see is good and clear."

Luke tried it, pointed them at Campbell.

"Hey!" he said, smiling.

"You got it, huh?"

"Yeah!"

"Good."

He turned the lenses out toward the field and focused again.

"Radical!"

Our Turtle friends again, thought David. He wondered who Luke's favorite was, Michelangelo or Do-
natello. Personally he leaned toward Leonardo,
though he guessed that basically Turtle Power was
Turtle Power. As opposed, for instance, to the Power
of Greyskull.

"You like 'em?"

"Yeah!"

"I'll loan them to you for the duration."

"What's a duration?"

"As long as you're here."

"And then I have to give them back again?"

"We'll see."

Luke looked hopeful. David guessed he was at that age when kids got very much into possessions.

"I'm gonna go look around, okay?"

"Go ahead."

He headed through the oak trees out into the field, stopped and turned and focused on the windows of the house. Campbell lit a cigarette and they watched him for a while.

"Seems like a nice boy," said Campbell.

"He is," said David.

"I'm not the sort of man who minds kids," said Campbell. "If he wants to hang around some when we start working it's okay by me. Sometimes it helps a boy to feel he's useful. 'Specially a boy with trouble."

"Trouble?"

He hadn't told Campbell a thing about Luke, or for that matter about Claire and Steven. Only that Luke was his godson and that he and Claire would be staying awhile.

"I've raised two boys and a girl myself, and I've built a lot of houses for a lot of people. Things come out in people when they're building houses. Things you sometimes don't really want to see. Stress, I guess you'd say. There's a lot of money involved, of course. House is a big investment. There's a lot of decisions that look small, but aren't. Not at the time. Hell, they're crucial. I'm not saying I've seen it all by now, but I did see a pretty good fella kick his dog one time just because his windows hadn't arrived the day we were ready to set 'em. Kids get trouble too. You see it sometimes."

It was the most he'd ever heard Campbell say on a subject. Any subject.

Campbell pulled on the Pall Mall and pointed to the deck above.

"We'll do this here in tongue-and-groove quarter-sawn fir," he said. "Soon as we finish the addition. You'll see. It'll look real nice."

Luke came to the edge of the clearing and put up the binoculars. The woods sprang into focus. Suddenly deep.

He wondered if it was okay to go in, if there were any bears in there. He wondered if bears could climb trees or if he just had to look for them along the ground.

Well, he was going in. He was an explorer, a scout looking for Indians or bear and he was going in.

He wouldn't go far.

The woods were cooler, damper. He liked the feel of the air in there, on his face and bare arms. He liked the green smell. He was glad he wasn't wearing shorts because in places the brush was thick and he had to plow through. He knew enough to watch for stickers and go around them. Sometimes if the brush wasn't *too* thick he'd jump right in and then crash through like you'd do if a bear were chasing you fast as a car. Then he'd come to a bunch of trees and slow down and there would be only the soft brown needles crackling under his Reeboks.

He was in a place like that now.

He was standing on a hill in a grove of pine trees and it was shady all around.

70

He raised the binoculars. He scouted the ground as far as he could see for Indians creeping through the brush below.

This was *fun*.

This was *scary*.

Partly it was scary because the game was scary, because Indians and bears were naturally scary, and partly it was the woods, because the woods was a wild place, a place he'd never been to before—and he *was* an explorer in a way. That part was real.

Something moved in the brush to his left; he heard the rustle, but by the time he turned and focused it was gone.

There were birds above him; he could hear them calling each other. He decided to try to find a nest. He was an explorer and he was starving in the wilderness and he needed the birds' eggs to keep him from dying.

Starving, he trudged forward to the very top of the hill.

Exhausted, he raised the binoculars. He scanned the trees.

He saw the platform immediately.

It was lodged between the branches of an oak tree the next hill over. The hill was a little bit higher than this one. He'd be able to see everything all around.

He forgot about starvation.

He ran down the hill until the ground turned mossy beneath him, slippery. Then he walked. He avoided a patch of stickers. The uphill climb was rocky and not too steep so his footing was good.

And there it was.

71

The treehouse was old—he didn't know how old but the wood was gray, weathered like David's porch. He wondered if it was safe. It was pretty high up. Maybe five times bigger than he was.

Scary.

He didn't want to fall.

The steps nailed to the tree trunk looked okay, though. The wood was thick and each step had two big nails hammered into it and none of the boards were cracked that he could see.

He'd start with the steps and see how it went.

The tree had grown at an incline, leaning slightly, so his climb wasn't hard. He didn't look down, just up to see if the next board above him seemed safe. There was one toward the top that was cracked at one end from the nail on over so he tugged on it to see if it would pull free. It didn't. He kept going.

Soon he was up.

There were four posts supporting a railing that went all the way around the platform at what looked like about waist level for him. He grabbed one of the posts and shook it. It wobbled a little, but it was pretty sturdy.

He looked for breaks in the platform flooring. There were leaves scattered around so he couldn't see it all, but what he could see didn't discourage him.

He hauled himself onto the platform.

He stood and squinted into the sunlight.

It was like being at the top of the world.

From here you could see all the way through the woods to David's house. He was a little surprised at how far away it was, how far he'd come. He raised the binoculars to see if he could spot David or Mr. Campbell but he couldn't, there were too many trees.

He looked down. And that surprised him too.

He really was way up there.

For some reason looking *out* was a whole lot better than looking down so that was what he did. He walked carefully to the other side of the platform, testing each step. The boards held. Through the trees the sky seemed to glint at him. He raised the binoculars again. He was amazed.

From here you could see the sea.

And now that he thought about it, you could smell it, too. Something salty and seaweedy coming toward him on the breeze. It reminded him somehow of the breath of a cat. Nice, but a little rotten.

It reminded him of the day his dad had taken him to Sandwich. They'd spent most of the day in a bar with a friend of his. Business, his dad had said—though it didn't sound like business. But then later in the day he'd let him go alone down to the ocean, to the rocks there, and look for crabs in the water. Maybe that was when they talked about business, he didn't know. He'd seen a couple of crabs he liked watching and when his father came to get him he didn't want to leave.

He cried. His dad had walked away from him.

He wondered how far away the ocean was from here. You couldn't tell exactly.

Thinking of his dad made him angry and sad the way it always seemed to do, a funny lonely feeling that made him want to punch or kick something. Like there was nobody around anywhere but him, just him, whether he was up in a treehouse really completely alone or sitting at his desk at school with his teacher and all the other kids around. And having to have that feeling, it wasn't fair at all. He knew he wasn't *really* alone. He knew it was dumb because his mom was always there, he had Ed and Tommy, he had friends, but there was still this stupid alone feeling and he still wanted to kick or hit something.

He didn't dare kick anything up here but maybe some leaves. Kicking a bunch of leaves wouldn't do him any good. But he did it anyway.

And something rattled across the platform.

Something white.

He squatted and sifted through the leaves.

Bones!

He didn't know what kind but they were bones, all right. Small, most of them, about the size of the bones of the model Tyrannosaurus that sat on his desk at home. Just a little dirty from being under the leaves, with some little red ants crawling over them.

He brushed away the ants. He collected the bones carefully one at a time and put them in his pocket. He got a pocketful.

He'd ask David what they were. David would know. Or Mr. Campbell.

Awesome!

What a neat place! *His* place. His *secret* place.

He grabbed the post and started down the ladder.

And got two steps down when something shook the tree above him.

He felt it on the ladder. A trembling in the tree itself. He froze there. Looking up.

74

A branch was swaying above the treehouse, maybe ten feet up. He couldn't see anything through the leaves. But something was there. Or had been.

Maybe it was gone now.

A squirrel or something.

And maybe it wasn't.

But the thrill of fear was there. That hadn't gone, it prickled the skin all over his body. And somehow that made the treehouse even better, that something had scared him there.

What a place!

He hurried down the ladder.

3:25 P.M.

"There's nothing I can do," said Claire. "He's on the *road* already."

Admittedly it was early. But the vodka tonic helped. And since Melissa was in for a nap now, Amy joined her.

"Where?"

"I don't know where. He wouldn't say. Just that he'd see us tonight. So we could talk. Jesus, the last thing I want to do tonight is to talk to Steven. Maybe two months ago I'd have wanted to. For Luke's sake if nothing else. But now . . ."

She heard Campbell's pickup pull out of the driveway. It made her feel strangely adrift, abandoned. She didn't even know the man except for ten minutes' talk in the kitchen. But he was normalcy, he was the regular stuff of David's and Amy's everyday life—one more person on their side, and by extension on *her* side. *It's crazy,* she thought. But she hated it that he was leaving.

"I don't get it," Amy said. "He doesn't want the divorce?"

"I don't know. He said he wants to talk about it. He's mad about something. He had that tone. Controlled. Edgy. Like he gets when he's holding something back that he doesn't want to deal with right away but he sure as hell will when the time comes. He'd been drinking."

"Good. Maybe he'll drive himself into a tree."

Claire reached for her drink. Her hand was shaking. She willed it steady.

"I don't want him to see Luke," she said. "He missed Christmas. He missed his *birthday*."

"You think Luke will want to see him?"

"I don't know. Probably. Probably he won't think about the last six months. He'll just be excited to see him again. He's his father."

And what nasty accident of genetics was that? she thought. That Luke should be such a decent kid, with such a father?

Oh, Luke was trouble. He was angry. He was defiant. Especially to her he was defiant lately. But partly that was his age and partly it was resentment and confusion over Steven being gone and the two of them being all alone together. Partly it was Luke feeling powerless to make things better. And partly it was her own fear. Her own frustration and anger ingested and absorbed by him.

He was angry all right. Yet there was a firm core of kindness in Luke, of caring and concern. You saw it in the way he'd looked at Melissa before. You saw it in the way he treated other kids. He wasn't a bully and he didn't appreciate kids who were. Though god knows he was big enough to qualify if he wanted to. He was even nice to the girls in his class.

At his age, that was something.

"You know he still has Steven's Christmas present wrapped in his room? A bird. A blue ceramic bird they made in school. It's absolutely terrible. He has to *tell* you it's a bird or you'd never know what it was. But he made it for Steven."

She was going to cry.

No you're not, she thought.

Amy helped, reached across the table and took her hand. The same gentle squeeze that had stopped the tears dozens of times over the years. Stopped them or started them flowing, as need be.

The back door opened and she started, afraid for a moment that it was Luke. She wasn't ready to see Luke yet, to have to talk to him about Steven. *I hate this,* she thought. *It's been* six months. *Am I supposed to let him see him now?*

But it was only David. He took one look at them and his smile faded. He stopped in the doorway.

"What's up?" he said.

"*Steven's* on his way," said Amy.

"What?"

"He just called half an hour ago."

David closed the door behind him. He went to the antique Coolerator, took out a beer and opened it. He closed the refrigerator door. He did all of these things carefully, as though door and refrigerator and bottle were all extremely fragile, as though they might break out of sheer molecular tension.

"What about the restraining order?" he said.

"He seems to be choosing to ignore it," said Amy.

"Oh yeah? The hell he is."

He went to the phone and started dialing.

"Who are you calling?"

"Vic Manetti. The police."

"Wait. Wait a minute," said Claire.

David looked at her. *He's a very nice man,* thought Claire, *and he cares. But I'm not at all sure about this.* He replaced the phone on the receiver and looked at her.

"What," he said.

"Luke," she said. "I'm thinking about Luke."

He walked to the table. She could feel his anger and indignation held tightly in check.

"What about Luke, Claire? Luke saw you backed against the kitchen wall one night while Steven worked off his drunk by slapping you around. Isn't that what the restraining order was about in the first place?"

"Yes."

"So what *about* Luke?"

"Steven's his father. It's been six months."

"So?"

"Luke misses him. He doesn't even talk about it anymore but that's just protective. He misses him anyway. I wish he didn't but he does. And I just don't know if I have the right to—"

"Of course you have the right. You have *every* right to—"

"Steven was drunk that night."

"He could be drunk right now," said Amy.

80

OFFSPRING

She felt suddenly exhausted. There was no denying
it. The voice on the phone was a drinker's voice, alternately slurred and too crisply under control. She
remembered the night in the kitchen, screaming for
Luke to get out of the room, to get back into bed, and
Luke running, terrified into total unnatural silence.
She remembered feeling Steven's physical presence
loom over her like the threat of bloody death or
worse, like a kind of rape, while he slapped her face
and punched her in the ribs and stomach and breasts,
targeting the breasts as though they had some sick
special meaning to him, knowing the meaning because for months he had not wanted to make love to
her, he had wanted to drink instead, and she had
asked him why that night, pleading for their marriage, not knowing he was drunk at first, and he was
telling her why, with each blow to her breasts he was
telling her why, that it was her womanness he
loathed, he hated, her unspeakable flesh.

"I'll call," she said.

"Let me," said David gently. He put his hand on
her shoulder. "I know some of these people."

He went back to the phone and dialed. Claire
looked at Amy, and Amy nodded to her, saying, it's
the right thing. It's the only thing. And squeezed her
hand again.

"Hello? Gloria? Is Vic there? It's David Halbard up
on River Road."

The air seemed suddenly stiller, the house quieter,
now that it was happening. Now that he was actually
calling the police to keep Steven away from them.

81

She remembered her dream last night. He was some sort of vampire or dog or snake. He was lying across her body and had pinned her to her bed. His teeth were in her neck. He was a dog and he started to pull back his head with her flesh in his teeth and shake.

The dog dream, in variations, went all the way back to her childhood. She would wake having peed the bed.

It was the first time the dog was Steven.

"Uh-huh? Okay. Well, we've got a kind of situation here as well. What it amounts to is we've got house-guests, a woman and her eight-year-old son. The woman's an old friend and she's involved in a very messy divorce right now. There's a restraining order against her husband.

"Yes, physical violence involved. He's not supposed to see them under any circumstances. None whatsoever. But now we've had a call from him saying he's on his way up here from Connecticut. He says he'll arrive tonight sometime. We don't know when or what the hell to do once he gets here."

He looked puzzled.

"What do you mean have I got a gun? Gloria, are you kidding?"

He listened, half smiling at first. They watched him. His voice got quieter.

"Can you give me any idea why?" he said. "I see. All right, we'll try it. But I'm not sure it'll do a whole lot of good. There'll be somebody there if we? . . . Okay . . . Thanks, Gloria. Take care, all right?"

He hung up, walked to the table, sat down, and drank his beer.

"That was truly *strange*," he said.

"What," said Amy.

"Gloria says that Vic and most of the sheriff's office are out investigating a murder. The state police are involved, too. They're strictly skeleton staff over there. I told her what we had and she said that, in the first place, they can't do anything until Steven actually arrives—which I guess I expected—but that if he insists on seeing Claire to call them, and that they'd 'try like hell to find somebody to send over,' was the way she put it. She said not to let him in the house if I could possibly help it, to try to talk him into turning around and going home again."

"What was that bit about the *gun?*"

"That was the weird part. Gloria's a bit flaky sometimes god knows and I don't know if she was just playing Miss Melodrama or what, but she actually suggested I order him off at gunpoint. Or anybody else I didn't know personally who came around tonight. Could you *see* me standing on the porch ordering Steven out of here, pointing a shotgun at him like . . . like Elvis in *Flaming Star*? Who the hell owns a gun? And even if we did . . ."

The screen door slammed. Claire jumped.

It was Luke. Beaming.

"Hey! Look, you guys! Look what I got!"

He was holding out his hand, coming toward her, and she might have scolded him for interrupting, some other time she probably would have, but somehow she *wanted* to be interrupted at the moment, with all this talk of guns and murder and with Steven coming and calling the police in the first place, so she smiled at him, what she hoped was a bright normal smile, and looked down into his hand at the tiny white bones that chance had arranged almost to correspond to *his* bones, to the bones of the palm of his hand splayed toward the fingers, as though she were looking inside him, into his flesh. At *him,* really. At frailty.

At mortality.

PART III

EVENING

5:35 P.M.

Steven Carey saw her on the bridge, backpack on the ground in front of her, just beyond the Kennebunk entrance to the highway.

It was rare you saw a girl hitching alone these days. He was in the slow lane doing sixty-five. His reactions were still very good. He pulled over.

Through the rearview mirror he saw her haul the heavy pack up onto her shoulder and run awkwardly toward the car. The weight of the pack made her run at an angle. It threw her balance off. She looked like the cat he'd run over one night after a high school dance. He'd been driving his father's old Pontiac. He'd stopped the car in the street to watch the cat in the headlights. The cat was leaking brain fluid and trying to run away, running at an angle.

He used a switch on the panel of the Mercedes' armrest to unlock the back door and another to roll

JACK KETCHUM

down the window on the frontseat passenger side. The girl appeared at the window and looked at him.

She looked wary. But you could see that she was impressed by the navy blue Paul Stuart suit and the darker blue Mercedes.

Blue was the color for inspiring trust in juries.

"Hi," he said. He smiled. "Put the pack in the back. Hop in."

The girl did as she was told. He watched her through the rearview mirror. She wasn't particularly pretty—nose a little too sharp, face a little too round. Eighteen or so and about ten pounds overweight. Thin brown hair. The usual jeans. And a pale green washed-out T-shirt that read, "Where the hell is Montserrat?" on the front and gave you a map of the Caribbean on the back.

She was strong. She handled the backpack well. And well mannered. She was careful not to slam the door.

She wore a bra.

They all did these days.

She got in front and he pulled away from the shoulder. He punched in the cigarette lighter and drew out a Winston.

"How far are you going?" she asked.

Her voice was breathy. He was disinclined toward breathy.

"Pretty much all the way up the coast," he said. He laughed. "Some godforsaken place called Dead River. You?"

"Portland."

He nodded. "There's an exit right off here."

90

"I know," she said. "Thanks." And finally she smiled. "Nice car," she said.

"Thank you."

There wasn't much traffic. He drove easily, carefully, edging it up to sixty-five again and no further.

The lighter hadn't popped. He pulled it out and it wasn't even warm. The goddamn thing was broken. He felt like throwing the goddamn thing out the goddamn window. He took a pack of matches out of his jacket pocket and lit the Winston.

It was getting on to dusk, and though he had no need of them yet, he switched on the headlights.

"What's in Portland?" he asked her.

She was biting at one of her fingernails. "My boyfriend goes to school there."

The girl had a boyfriend.

The girl was getting laid.

The girl took off the bra and the boyfriend sucked her nipples.

"You're a student too?" he asked.

"I quit for a year. I wanted to work for a while. I go back in September."

"Sure. Plenty of time for work," he said.

She nodded. "I guess."

Plenty of time, he thought. *I ought to know.* Military academy to college to law school to practice practice *practice . . .*

She bit her nail again.

Marion did that.

A very bad habit.

He had caught her doing it this very morning, sit-

91

ting in bed with the sheet up over her lap, leaning down squinting at her stocks listed in the morning paper so that her long thin breasts lay over the roll of fat in her middle and her tousled black hair hung over her face. She was chewing at the nail of the index finger of her left hand, and when she bit it off she put it in the ashtray next to her Virginia Slim Menthol Light.

He saw her doing this just as he stepped out of the shower, and he was already wondering what to do with her by then, in fact he'd been wondering since the night before when she told him they would no longer be able to use him at the firm past the end of the month, either on or off the books, that the plan to rehire him was scotched now once and for all because Linfield had seen him in the office last week and Linfield was complaining to her as senior partner that here was this person still working for them who had lost him a fucking bundle, and what in the hell was he doing there. He would not forget. He would not be convinced or mollified and Mr. Cocksucker B. Linfield was their third fucking biggest client. Sorry.

He was thinking what to do about her—about someone who wanted his cock in the dark of night but had no allegiance and no honor while the cigarette burned and the fingernail smoldered in the ashtray. He could smell it. The smell of burning flesh. She was naked and fat and checking her stocks in the newspaper.

His hands gripped the steering wheel. He eased them, flexed the fingers.

The girl was frowning.

"You know? I think I know Dead River," she said. "Isn't that up near Lubec? Way up near the border?"

"I don't know about Lubec, but it's nearly all the

way to Canada, all right. Actually I've never been there. I just looked at the map and figured you could take Ninety-five up to around Brunswick and then cut over to Highway One, past Boothbay Harbor on up." He flashed her a grin. "Sound about right?"

She nodded. "I have an older cousin who used to work the fishing boats up that way every summer. Earned himself some money for college. That's why it's familiar.

"It's pretty nice country. Why didn't you just fly?"

"Fly?"

"Sure. I mean, it's a really long drive. You could have flown to Machias. At least that far. And I think there might even be a little airport around Lubec. I don't remember." She smiled shyly. "I mean, you don't look like you'd have a whole lot of trouble affording it, you know?"

He laughed. He stubbed out the Winston.

"The problem is I'm a nervous flyer. I hit a downdraft coming home into Kennedy one time that scared the hell out of me. Once burned, twice shy, you know? That kind of thing."

They like it when you appear vulnerable, he thought. Even though in this case the downdraft story was true.

"Kennedy? You've come all the way up from New York?"

"Connecticut, actually. I was visiting . . . a friend there."

"Oh."

He had to be careful. He was giving her too much information. He was already memorable. The suit, the red silk tie, the Mercedes.

93

JACK KETCHUM

He probably should not have picked her up in the first place. He'd wanted the company.

It gave him an idea.

"Listen. Maybe you could help me out here." He smiled his most disarming smile and shook his head. "The thing of it is, I really don't know *where* the hell I'm going and I'm hopeless reading road signs at night. What would you say to driving up with me? Ride shotgun. Just get me up there. Then I'd drive you over to the airport at Machias or Lubec or wherever and put you on a plane back to Portland." He laughed. "That is assuming you aren't afraid of flying too. On my tab, naturally. And I'll give you fifty, seventy-five dollars for your trouble. It's going to get dark in a couple hours. You'd really be helping me out. What do you say?"

The girl just looked at him, caught completely by surprise. Well, he was a stranger after all. He guessed she would be.

"I . . ."

"What time are you supposed to be there? Is there anybody you could call to say you'd be a little later than expected? Your boyfriend? We could stop at a pay phone somewhere. Call's on me of course. I'd really appreciate it. You said it was pretty country."

"But how could I . . . ? I mean, Portland's less than an hour from here."

"So?"

"Dead River has to be two hundred miles up the coast. More, probably. It'll be nine or ten o'clock before you even get there. By the time I got a plane back to Portland, even if I was *lucky* it'd be midnight!"

He laughed. "Think of it as an adventure."

94

She stared at him.

Staring was rude. The girl wasn't as well mannered as he'd thought.

He honestly couldn't see why it should be such a terribly big deal to her. It was only a couple of hours. A nice pleasant drive in the country. He'd picked her up, hadn't he? Given her a ride? Didn't she owe him a little something?

"Make it a hundred," he said. "Think about it."

She flinched as he reached abruptly across her lap to the glove compartment and pulled out the bottle. Her flinching amused him.

Skittish little thing.

He offered her the vodka. He smiled.

"Let me buy you a drink," he said.

She shook her head.

"Oh, come on. You don't want to force me to drink alone, do you? What's your name, by the way?"

He unscrewed the cap on the bottle.

"S-Susan."

"Susan. That's a nice name. Suzie. Suzie Cream-cheese. Lazy Susan. Suzerain. Suzerain means feudal lord, did you know that? Someone to whom allegiance is due. Let's see. Oh Susannah. Sweet Sue. He ever call you that? Your boyfriend? Sweet Sue?"

He drank.

"I . . . I think I'd like to . . . get out now," she said. "Stop anywhere, okay?"

"Out?"

"Yes."

"You're going to Portland, aren't you?"

"Yes, but . . ."

"You want to get out?"

"Yes."

"Why?"

"You're drinking."

"That's true. I am."

He drank again. *Fuck her,* he thought. She was either going with him or she wasn't, and either way she was going nowhere.

It had been a very bad day, he reflected. And obviously it wasn't getting any better because the goddamn fucking girl was giving him trouble and would probably continue to give him trouble and the lighter didn't work.

The day had been very bad in one way. And very good in another.

It had been a long time, he thought. A real long time indeed.

Not since Jimmy whatsisname. Over on Livingston Avenue.

They'd been playing in the apple orchard, a bunch of them he recognized from school. What was it, third grade? Right. They'd been playing soldier, using the little green apples fallen from the trees for grenades, tossing them and falling flat into the tall grass, hiding, crawling toward one another like troops in combat. Nobody had heard him approach and nobody had seen him. And at first nobody knew that the rocks he was throwing were not just the same little green apples they all were using. Not until one of them hit Jimmy in the head and he went down bleeding.

And died in a coma. They never knew that he was the one throwing the rocks and he never told them.

He was good at secrets. And there was no point in them knowing anyway because Jimmy was dead.

And now there was no good reason for them knowing about Marion either because Marion was dead too, the victim of a prowler who in the early-morning hours had strangled her with the cord of her hair dryer and had then stolen her stereo and CD player, her television and jewelry—all of it smashed and scattered in a dump outside of Hartford, Connecticut.

Again, nobody had seen him.

Her cleaning lady had been there the day before and she was very thorough so he had no particular worry about fingerprints. He knew the routine. He'd wiped off everything he touched. He had a very good memory for incidentals.

And they'd kept their affair quite secret.

Marion had insisted on it. A matter of office decorum.

He had done it very calmly. Not so much out of anger as because she had deserved to die for feeling free to so easily betray him. And because he *wanted* to.

She was fat and her breasts were long and ugly and he wanted to.

That was the good part of the day and it was very good indeed.

There had been no slipups, he was sure of that. No police would be knocking at his door. He had gone to work in the usual way with the television and jewelry and all the rest of it in the trunk of his car and accomplished much, and only became agitated when Claire's lawyer served him the papers, right there in full view of most of the staff.

97

It was completely normal, unremarkable behavior. You were being divorced, you got agitated.

No one would suspect him of a thing.

He wondered if they'd found her yet.

He'd been careful to rape the body afterward, just for authenticity's sake. He'd been surprised, actually, at the size of his hardon. Better than she'd managed to do for him in life as far as he could remember. But it was really the one-two-three punch he was after. *Assault, theft, rape.* You saw it every day. The police would be looking for a thief with priors of sexual offense and they wouldn't tend to look much further.

"So what do you think?" he said.

"About what?"

"About driving with me."

The girl's voice had gotten smaller, even breathier. He liked that. It meant she respected him.

Claire's voice was deep, almost masculine.

He was going to see Claire. He was going to have to talk to her.

"I'm visiting my wife and son, if that's your problem. I'm a married man. Look."

He showed her the ring.

"I . . . I've got to get to Portland. I'm expected, you know?"

"When?"

"In . . . in about an hour."

The girl was lying. She was hitching. The time would depend on the rides. They wouldn't know when to expect her.

He drank from the bottle.

"So you don't want to go with me? You won't do me a favor?"

"I can't."

"Sure you can. You just don't *want* to. Might as well say it. Go ahead. Tell me you just don't want to."

"I . . ."

"Say, 'I just don't want to.' "

"I . . ."

She was scared now. Really scared. The girl was shitting her pants over there.

"*Say* it!"

"I don't want to!"

He smiled. "That's better. Now you're telling me the truth. Okay. Get out."

It was getting on to dusk. There was one car well ahead of him and another far behind. He checked the speedometer. He was still doing a little under sixty-five.

"Go on," he said. "Get out."

"You have to . . . you've got to pull over."

"No I don't. Get out. Go on. Get the fuck out."

He was calm, smiling. He took another drink of the vodka. He glanced at the girl. The girl was crying. That was okay. At least she wasn't being too noisy about it.

"I . . . can't . . ."

"Okay. Throw your pack out, then."

"Huh?"

He used the button on the armrest to unroll the rear passenger-side window.

"Throw your pack out the window and I'll pull over. I promise."

"Why? . . . Why do you want to do that?"

"I just do. You want me to pull over? Then throw it out the window."

At first he thought maybe she was *too* scared, that she wasn't going to do it, that all she was going to do was sit there looking at him. But then she must have thought better about it because she leaned over the seat and started to haul up the heavy pack and finally she had it halfway out the window and was pushing at it to get it through when he reached over and cupped her breast and squeezed it, not too hard, and she froze there, still holding on to the backpack, eyes squinted shut, crying.

He squeezed harder.

"Push it," he said quietly. And the girl did push, and the pack spilled out the window.

He released her.

Through the rearview mirror he watched it tumble, bouncing high behind them, its aluminum frame crumbling, the pack exploding open on the shoulder, her clothes, books, papers—whatever—flying everywhere.

He laughed until the pack was just a tiny speck behind them.

He slowed and pulled over.

He used the button on the armrest to unlock her door.

The girl looked amazed. She hesitated. *Was she actually free?* He wondered if she would retain the presence of mind to read and remember his license plate. He doubted it.

She flung the door open and hurled herself outside.

"Portland welcomes you," he said. "Have a very nice day."

A car whizzed past him. He pulled out onto the highway.

I'm coming, Claire, he thought.

It's payback day.

7:50 P.M.

She squatted, sharpening the knife in the twilight gloom just inside the entrance to the cave, a slit in the rock draped with sphagnum moss thirty-five feet above the sea.

Outside gulls cried and high tide pummeled the rocks.

She sharpened the knife with a shard of Carborundum, stolen many years ago and kept in a pouch tied to her belt so it was always near at hand, coarse on one side and fine on the other, grinding the edge in a circular movement, tilting the blade to grind toward the knife point, giving it a feather edge, then pushing the edge straight across the stone, turning it over to push the other side forward too, smoothing away the feather. She did this perfectly and without having to think.

Instead the Woman's thoughts flew over each of them inside like a flock of keen-eyed birds, knowing each crag and crevice of her landscape, detecting the

103

slightest change there. She surveyed her family and—despite the foolishness of children—did not find them wanting.

She looked at the man sorting through a pile of knives, axes, ax handles, screwdrivers, claw hammers, hatchets and other tools and weapons along the far wall beside their small, nearly smokeless hardwood fire. The man was choosing in an orderly manner, laying out the weapons, knowing what each would do tonight and what he or she would need.

There were guns, too, in the pile—shotguns, rifles, pistols. They had long ago run out of bullets and shells. They kept them anyway.

She watched his hard body move in the rich glow of the fire.

In First Stolen she had chosen well.

She had seen his ghost immediately.

His ghost was strong.

The kitten was on a string. The boy would drag the string into the pounding surf until the kitten screamed and tumbled over itself in the waves and then he would allow the string some slack, let the kitten return to the shoreline for a moment, then repeat the process until the kitten's eyes were dazed and it no longer cared to scream. The boy did not laugh, did not seem to enjoy the game. Only watched.

Night had only just fallen and he was playing alone by the shoreline.

At her approach he looked up and she knew he was upset to be caught with the kitten that way.

He started to talk. Like all of them he talked too much. Trying to distract her from what he was doing with the kit-

ten. Asking her questions. What was her name. Where did she come from. Saying that he was staying with his parents on the big house on the hill, pointing to it, saying he hated the house and hated his parents, saying to her defiantly that the kitten was his to do with as he liked.

She smiled. She picked up the kitten and walked into the water and held it under.

It had scratched her only a little.

That was eleven years ago, only months after the Night of First Tears, and the wound in her side was still draining despite the poultice she had made from the raw linings of eggshells and her diet of stolen moldy bread.

The boy was curious about the wound and asked her questions as they walked along the shoreline.

She knew she would have to teach him not to talk so much and not to ask questions. It would not be hard. At fifteen summers, she was his elder by four summers and despite the wound she was stronger than he was and knew that she would always be stronger.

She watched him now select the largest ax and set it aside for himself against the wall of the cave, then return to the pile and tuck a claw hammer into his frayed belt. The hammer and ax were always his weapons of choice.

He was naked to the waist. His man's body had formed strongly. She looked at his body. She remembered teaching him.

At twelve summers he was a father. She had borne his first child, the Girl, on a bed of seaweed at the shoreline. It was night and the moon was full just as it was tonight.

The Woman still was teaching him.

She ran the flat of the sharp blade over her naked breasts, down across her thighs, and between her legs as she thought of him.

The Girl, their daughter, sat beside him in front of the fire, picking lice from the heads of the twin males who had been born the summer after her. She flicked the lice into the fire.

The lice sizzled, threw thin wisps of smoke.

A ring of clear faceted stone that sparkled in the firelight dangled from a cord around the Girl's neck. A necklace of bones hung lower. There were egret, owl, and gull's feathers tied into her long dark hair.

More than any of them the Girl cared for adornment.

The Girl wore breasts, the skin stretched low and tight and tied around her middle. The breasts had been taken many years ago. They were deep yellow in color and cracked in many places, particularly across the left nipple where the skin had nearly worn through. But the Girl had no breasts of her own yet. She wore them proudly.

She frowned, fussing over the lice in the twin males' hair. The males ignored her, concentrating instead on the greasy bones that were all that remained of last night's feast.

Their only other child together, the Boy, a male of six summers, played with the Cow deep in the shadows of the cave, tormenting the Cow with a rusted fireplace poker, jabbing it in the ribs. The Cow bucked and strained against its chains.

The Boy was able to see out of his right eye only and held his head at an angle. His left eye had been clouded by a hornet's sting shortly after the Woman bore him and it had never become clear again.

The Boy had been tormenting the Cow for some time now. The Boy was stronger than he thought himself to be. The Cow would be bruised all along its rib cage tomorrow. It bellowed.

It was not unusual for the Boy to play with the Cow in this manner but Second Stolen had perhaps grown tired of hearing it bellow for a while because she walked to the boy and took his poker and whacked him with it once across the bottom. The Boy looked up at her resentfully but did not cry . . . though now he too would have a bruise tomorrow.

He ran to Eartheater and soon they were playing on the floor of the cave, tossing the sun-bleached bones of a rat in some game they had invented together and which none of the others but the Boy, Eartheater and Rabbit had ever understood.

The Woman did not mind that Second Stolen had disciplined the Boy. The fact that he was her son and not Second Stolen's made no difference to her. To her they all were the same. Her children by First Stolen were the same to her as Rabbit, her son of seven summers by the Cow. And Rabbit was the same as Eartheater—so called because she would eat anything, even handfuls of earth when she was hungry—the daughter of the union between First and Second Stolen. And Eartheater was the same to her as Second Stolen's infant daughter by the Cow, sleeping now in the browse bed made of pine boughs by the fire.

There was no disgrace in having been fathered by the Cow. That was what the Cow was for.

As Second Stolen was using him now.

The Woman smiled. Clearly it had not been the Cow's bellowing that made Second Stolen chase the Boy away—but this.

The Woman had no concept of beauty.

She herself was not beautiful. Not unless power was beauty, because she was powerful, over six feet tall, with long arms and legs, almost simian in their lean strength. But her wide gray eyes were empty when they were not watchful and she was pale from lack of light, filthy as they all were filthy, parasite and insect bitten and smelling of blood like a vulture. A wide smooth scar ran from just below her full right breast to just above her hip where eleven years ago one of the shotgun blasts had peeled her flesh away. Over her left eye and extending an inch beyond her ear, a second blast had left another scar. Neither her eyebrow nor her hair from forehead to the back of her ear had ever grown in again.

She looked as though struck by lightning.

The Woman was not beautiful, and had no concept of beauty. But she recognized a certain delicacy in Second Stolen. A mastery of the Cow that was almost beauty and to her as pleasing.

She watched the familiar ritual.

The Cow whimpered as Second Stolen approached—as he had whimpered nearly every day of the eight full summers they had used him.

Whether the Cow whimpered in anticipation of pain or pleasure the Woman had never known and did not care.

108

Second Stolen had just bathed. It was the first she had bathed in a very long time, but it was necessary. Both she and the Cow were naked. The Cow was always naked.

His breath was coming faster, his chest heaving.

She watched Second Stolen grip the slack flesh of his belly and twist it for her pleasure, and then reach down.

Second Stolen milked the Cow.

The Cow began to rise.

The Cow was much older than the Woman, yet he could be counted upon to rise quickly—even more quickly than First Stolen, who sometimes allowed himself to become distracted from their need of him. But the Cow had no mind and no distractions. As though the milking were necessary to him.

She watched Second Stolen wrap her legs around his back, grasp his shoulders and trap him inside her.

In a matter of moments she shuddered. They were finished.

It was good, thought the Woman, that she had taken the moment to use the Cow. Second Stolen's part would be hard tonight. There was pain in it. And Second Stolen had already had pain. She had taken it upon herself when she had failed to find the children the night before and then received it again from the Woman and First Stolen, when they knew what the children had done.

Not even the spoils of the hunt could allow her to forgive what the children had done. Each had received a beating. Second Stolen's most severe because at seventeen summers she was the eldest and had failed to find and stop them.

The infant's ghost haunted her. Even now.

The children had been impatient for her to know them as hunters on their own. The Woman knew how dangerous that was. It had been the reason for her family's destruction eleven summers ago. And somehow last night she had felt another disaster moving toward them through the clouds, that the children were not just chasing down a rabbit or running after land crabs in the moonlight but were involved in another kind of hunt entirely. A hunt fraught with peril.

She sheathed her knife. She glanced at the still white bag isolated in the far corner of the cave opposite the Cow and felt a sudden chill.

In a sense it had been her fault. She had spoken to them far too often for far too many days and nights about the other child—the one on the hill—and of the power in the blood of children. It had made them impatient. She knew that now.

So they had taken this other child and the mother and the girl.

They had not meant to, but they had done so in the worst possible way.

The child had died *inside* the bag. Because it could not breathe.

No blood had been spilled.

No blood *released*.

And it was release that held the power. To release the blood was to release the ghost and the power of the ghost. And though the body might struggle, the ghost was always thankful for it.

While this ghost lay in a bag filled only with the body of a child and the child's shit and urine. Angry, trapped inside its body.

The ghost was a danger to them now.

A ghost so young it had barely lived. It would be filled with resentment toward them, filled to bursting.

There was no appeasement possible. The harm was accomplished. It could only be thrust out to sea now, to drift far away from them on the tides.

They would go north again after tonight. The tide would draw the body south.

And tonight they would take power from the other infant. For their journey. To strengthen the Woman and her family.

And tomorrow night they would leave here.

The cave was good, but caves were many.

It was time.

She gestured to First Stolen. He came forward and stood beside her. The others stopped what they were doing and watched, knowing and expectant. Only Rabbit smiled. But then Rabbit was a fool whose brains had formed no more properly than his brown-pitted teeth.

Rabbit was always smiling.

His ruined teeth made her irritable. She preferred the ones the Girl had fashioned for each of the children, strange and ugly as they were, thin and multicolored, to Rabbit's real ones.

The Woman gestured to Second Stolen and she came forward too, and stood between them. She turned so that she presented her back to them and raised her arms above her head.

Her back, buttocks and thighs were dark with crusted blood and some of the wounds had opened since bathing.

"No," said the Woman. This was not punishment, this was the hunt. It made other demands upon Second Stolen, and though they were alike they were not the same. And Second Stolen knew this. But because the demands of the hunt were more painful, she had been reluctant to face them.

She turned and faced them now.

She raised her arms again, while the Woman and First Stolen each took thin birch switches off the floor of the cave.

She did not cry out as the switches slashed across her belly, thighs, neck and shoulders—even across her face, though they were careful not to harm the eyes and ears, and careful too of the nipples of her breasts for the sake of the suckling baby. Nor did she try to move away. Yet the Woman saw her pain. It was good to give pain and good to receive pain because that was what life was, and Second Stolen knew the reason for this pain and that it was a good thing, that it had to be.

The children watched, learning.

The Cow rattled his chains.

When it was finished all three were sweating in the humid heat of the cave and Second Stolen stood before them washed with blood as though they had painted her body with the juices of berries—except that the wounds were visible too as was necessary and their switches dripped with blood.

They needed only their weapons now.

OFFSPRING

She slipped into the torn checkered shirt they had taken from the fisherman long ago; the one she had beheaded with a single perfect stroke of the ax to show First Stolen how well and swiftly it should be done. The fisherman's knife she wore sheathed in her belt.

The children rose and walked to the pile and in moments they were ready.

PART IV

NIGHT

8:20 P.M.

They walked the beach. Beneath their feet the sand gleamed in the moonlight, studded with stones.

The Woman knew this place.

Not far from them lay the cave where they had lived on the Night of First Tears.

Across the channel, invisible in the dark, was the island where she was born.

She remembered it dimly. She remembered that they had hidden for many days, had finally been driven away by men with guns searching for those other men they had taken for the hunt. The Woman had not known about guns then, though her elders understood the threat and had fled to the mainland.

She remembered that fish were abundant on the island, and birds, and that while true feasts occurred only rarely, the hunting was always safe.

Now that she was elder and leader of her family,

117

the hunting was never safe. Guns were everywhere. Planning was necessary, and caution.

First Stolen liked to pretend that because he was the eldest male he was leader. But First Stolen had no caution and could not plan. He had never been leader. He could never be. It was only pride and foolishness that made him walk one step ahead of her as he did now, his ax slung across his shoulder. In many ways First Stolen was still a child.

Second Stolen, walking naked beside her, was wiser.

There was a calm about Second Stolen, an acceptance of things. An ability to wait and reason.

It had not always been that way. For the entire cycle of the first moon of her captivity, the Woman had been forced to keep her tied in the dark in a hole at the back of the cave and had beaten her each day because she cried so often for her mother—though, strangely, never for her father—even though she already had six summers by then and should have been stronger.

Over time the crying stopped. And then it was as though she had always been there.

The Woman gazed out to sea. It was high tide now, as it had been the night her family fled the island.

That family was gone, destroyed. And now it was back again.

She had rebuilt them. They were strong.

The children ranged across the beach to either side of her. Rabbit—the best hunter among them despite his stupidity about other things, in the lead—then the twin males, followed by the Girl, Eartheater, the

Boy with the clouded eye. Only the infant had been left behind.

She felt the power of them swell and surge inside her.

Her family had been like the seaweed at low tide— Shriveled by the sun, black with ruin, dry almost to the point of breaking. Then the sea rose up again, filling them, turning them green and supple and alive.

The sea was blood.

The night crashed with surf, in her ears a brilliant thunder.

8:45 P.M.

"It's no good," Manetti said. "It's gotten too damn dark. Somebody's just going to wind up busting his skull on these rocks here."

He was right, thought Peters. The search was hampered by high tide now, the beach shrunk to a narrow strip of sand, forcing them back toward the granite cliffs and the erosion spill of rocks beneath, which were already slippery from the spray of surf. The waves filled crevices and tide pools. They were stepping around them, stepping over them. Peters' hair and clothes were damp with spray. He tasted salt on his lips. The men were exhausted.

Enough was enough.

At this angle, having to stand this close to the rock face, they weren't going to find a damn thing anyhow. You couldn't tell what was a cave—never mind how deep a cave, whether it was deep enough to live in—and what was just a fissure or a cleft in the rock.

The troopers had provided them with heavy, three-foot-long Maglite Six-Cells—which went for forty dollars a pop thank you very much—but their bright beams just slashed straight up the sea-wall, and everything looked pretty much the same as everything else. It was like looking for a nail hole in your bedroom wall with your face pressed up against the baseboard. You just couldn't do it.

"Might as well call it in all across the board," said Peters. "I don't guess anybody's having much more luck than we are."

"Damn!" said Harrison. He'd been scanning the rock face and walking at the same time. He'd stepped into a tide pool, and now his shoe was full of seawater.

In Peters' boyhood they'd called it a soaker.

Manetti took out his radio and made the call. All units proceed to stage-two planning. Effective immediately.

Stage two was house-to-house.

It would take some time to get organized—hell, it would take them a while just to get off the beach—but each unit had its own territory mapped out already all along the coastline. They had orders not to alarm anybody but to alert *everybody*. Stay indoors, keep telephone and radio lines open, keep doors and windows locked, and call the police to inform them of anything unusual whatsoever.

They'd probably be at it all night.

He'd been up since half past three this morning and by now he was beyond tired, even beyond exhausted, he was into some realm of autopilot wherein half of what he looked at just didn't look right. It was as though he were this close to getting lost all the time, saying to himself, okay, now where the hell am I? Even though he knew this coast like he knew his own front porch.

He kept seeing things move out of the corner of his eye, people-sized things, and when he turned and looked there was nothing there.

It wasn't the booze. That was long gone.

There was a spare bottle left in the glove compartment of his car, half-full, that he kept there for emergencies but the car was home and they were heading for Manetti's cruiser. He wondered if Manetti'd want to make a pit stop. He sort of doubted it.

They were trudging across a strip of sand. It was a welcome relief from the slick rocks. Harrison and the four troopers were leading now, Manetti and Peters a few feet behind. Manetti looked at him. *Here we go again,* he thought. He knew what he looked like.

"You want to call it a night, George, I'll understand."

"I want like all hell to call it a night. But I don't guess I will just yet. I guess if I slip into a coma you can just leave me in the cruiser."

"What's your guess? You figure they'll stay home tonight, watch television? Or are they out hunting again?"

"I'd say hunting. Why waste a moon like that in front of the TV?"

They walked quietly for a long time.

Then there it was again. A figure moving alongside of him.

123

The little man who wasn't there.

He needed a second wind right about now and needed it bad.

Peters sighed. "Our territory's the Point, right?"

"Right."

"Listen. That's by my house. Mind dropping me off a minute? I'd feel a little more comfortable with the .38 around."

Worth a try, he thought.

Manetti just looked at him again. He'd caught his own tone of voice and knew he wasn't fooling anybody. But Manetti wasn't calling him on it. He nodded.

"Sure, George."

It was a big concession, he knew. Cops weren't supposed to drink on duty. Civilians weren't supposed to drink and carry handguns.

Peters wasn't exactly a cop anymore. But at the moment he wasn't exactly a civilian either. He wondered if that meant he was breaking two laws or none. He guessed Manetti had judged it to be none. Or maybe he hadn't wanted to judge it at all.

And how do you judge it? he thought.

He was much too tired. He came up empty.

Miles Harrison found the path. He turned to Peters and smiled.

"We used to come down here as kids," he said. "Light fires on the beach. Neck. Have a beer or two."

"I know," Peters said. "I used to come down here to arrest you."

Harrison laughed. "You never did, though."

"I never wanted to. I just wanted you off the beach.

What did you think we came parading down here waving lighted flashlights for?"

"I guess we just figured the cops were pretty dumb."

"We were. And now you are. All cops are dumb, remember?"

"We always came back a night or two later."

"And we'd chase you again. I know."

They were on the uphill path now and Peters' breath was coming hard, he was puffing.

"I always thought we were just lucky," Harrison said. "Not to get caught I mean."

Peters stopped and looked at him, took a breath.

"You were lucky," he said.

Damn lucky, he thought. *Luckier than you know, given what was out here.* They proceeded up the mountain.

9:15 P.M.

"Wait a minute! Wait a minute! I can't . . ."

"Get into *bed*, Luke. Now!"

There was always trouble around bedtime and obviously tonight was going to be no exception.

Claire didn't know whether to throw up her hands or throttle him.

The fact that the room was new to him didn't help. He'd scattered his guys—his Turtle guys, his Dick Tracy guys—all over the place playing up here tonight, and now he couldn't find anything.

So he stood there in his pajamas, scowling.

Getting him into *those* had been a major event too. He'd insisted on wearing the same dirty T-shirt he'd been wearing all day, his favorite, the Post Nukes T-shirt he'd picked out for himself in California, a skeleton riding a surfboard against a lurid flaming red sky.

Then there were five full minutes of Did You Brush Your Teeth.

And now he stood there jiggling his legs back and forth as though he had to go to the bathroom. He didn't. He'd already gone.

It was just bedtime. No matter what time it rolled around it was always too early for him. He was wired to the gills. Half-whiny, half-tyrant.

Eight-year-old boys, she thought. *Give me strength.*

"I can't help it! I gotta find *Flattop!* I'm not getting into bed until I find him. You can't make me. It's not my fault . . ."

Mouth going a mile a minute. She wondered if he even knew what he was saying when he got like this.

The child from hell.

She normally let him play himself to sleep. Once he got under the covers it didn't take long for him to drift away. The problem was getting him horizontal.

"You can live without Flattop for tonight, Luke. Get into bed."

"No, see, I gotta . . ."

"I'm not going to say it again."

"But I *need* Flattop!"

"One."

"Mom!"

Close to tears now.

"Two."

Crying. *My god!* she thought. The drama!

"You *hate* me!"

"I do not hate you, Luke. But if I reach the number three and you're not in bed you will not see daylight for a week. Do you understand me? Now what number did I just say?"

128

"Two."

Just standing there. Pushing it right to the limit.

"All right. Th . . ."

Then flinging himself into bed. She hoped they weren't listening to this downstairs. She hoped they had good bedsprings.

"Three. Thank you very much, Luke. Thank you for making that so very easy."

That sardonic little smile.

He enjoys this, she thought. *He's having some kind of weird power-game good time.*

While she felt frazzled.

"I love you, Mommy. I hate you, Mommy." He laughed. "Just kidding."

Claire sighed. She sat down on the bed beside him.

"Listen to me, Luke. I want us to have a nice day tomorrow. I want you to be a good boy just like you were almost all day today, and not give me, or David, or Amy, a hard time. I want you to be cooperative. Do you understand?"

He nodded.

"And no more of this like tonight. If we go through this again tomorrow night you're grounded. No television. No playing outside. Clear?"

"Uh-huh."

"Okay. Your guys are right here on the floor. Give me a kiss, honey."

He smiled and kissed her. A nice little boy again. The weirdness and wiredness gone.

Jekyll and Hyde, Jr.

She gave him a hug.

"I love you, honey."

"Love you too, Mommy."

She got up and turned out the light. The light in the hall, though it was dim, would be all he'd need to play by.

"I'll be right next door, okay? And you know where the bathroom is, right?"

"Uh-huh."

She closed the door a little. Not too much.

" 'Night. I love you."

" 'Night."

She heard him scoop his guys off the floor and begin his night's scenario, speaking softly in strange voices behind her.

She walked next door to her room and sat on the bed. The urge to sleep was strong. But David and Amy were downstairs, holding a movie for her on the VCR. They'd watched it halfway through already but Claire barely knew what it was about. It wasn't the movie's fault.

It was waiting for Steven.

Thinking what to say.

Wondering whether she should wake Luke up or not.

That was why she'd wanted him to go to bed so badly in the first place. This way at least she had control—she had a choice.

She looked at her watch. It was twenty after nine.

It probably wouldn't be long now.

She felt completely unprepared for him.

She already had a headache.

She'd brought some aspirin. They were around here somewhere. It made her aware that she was in a strange room too, just like Luke.

130

She pictured Luke on the bed. That look. Testing her.
I love you, Mommy. I hate you, Mommy.
Just kidding.

The problem was that he wasn't kidding. Or that he was kidding less than he knew.

Of course he loved her. And of course he hated her, too. From his point of view she had to be at least one-half the reason they weren't a family anymore. And because she was still there and Steven wasn't, hers was the half that grated. He could forget about Steven for long stretches of time. He couldn't forget about her so easily. Day by day she was there to remind him that somehow their family had failed, and by extension that *he* had failed—to be important enough to link them all together—that he had no power, ultimately, to affect his future. She was the image of his disenfranchisement.

Yet he loved her. Sometimes to both their distractions. She'd read that even kids from solid, happy families focus very strongly on their mothers at his age, demanding much. Constant attention, constant *conversation*, continual approval.

Haunting her.

And at the same time resisting her.

She got up and found the aspirin in the side pocket of her suitcase. She swallowed three of them, wishing they were Advil instead. The aspirin tasted grainy and bitter.

With Luke the anger could surface like a sudden storm.

A few weeks after his birthday he'd wanted her to buy him some new Turtle guy at K-Mart. She was pinching pennies that week just to come up with the grocery money. And he'd just had a birthday after all, with plenty of presents. She said no. So Luke started shrieking about her not loving him and not caring if he was happy or unhappy, overreacting like crazy, and even after she got him quiet and got herself quiet, it hurt that the thought had even crossed his mind.

It wasn't her doing. It was Steven's. When she was sane, she knew that. She was working hard here, doing her damnedest to hold things together.

But it wasn't Luke's fault either. And Luke was suffering.

The way he walked, a little hunched over, looking down at the ground half the time. The much-too-frequent scowl. The urge to be so damned ingratiating even to the creepiest kids at school, the ones who had real problems. Violent problems, some of them.

It all added up to a kid who didn't think much of himself these days.

It added up to a victim.

And we're not much different there, she thought.

Victim.

She'd thought hard on that word.

She'd gone so far as to look it up once, found that it came from the word *weik,* having to do with magic and casting spells—with wizards and witches—and then to do with tricksters, with guile and cunning.

She remembered smiling at the time. Because in its odd way the older word fit what Steven had done to them as perfectly as the meaning that had evolved from it.

She thought she knew what she would do in regard to Steven.

A boy did not need to be twisted like that. Not even by his father. Lastly by his father.

She didn't need it, either.

She turned off the bedroom light and went down to join David and Amy.

Like normal people, to watch a movie.

In the dim light from the hall Dick Tracy flattened Pruneface with his nightstick and the game was over, even though Pruneface was armed to the teeth with machine gun, pistol, knife and bludgeon, proving once again that the law was the law and bad guys didn't get away with crossing it.

Unless you were Freddy Krueger or somebody.

His mother couldn't stand Freddy Krueger.

She'd yelled at him again tonight. She yelled at him a lot lately.

He supposed that a lot of times he deserved it because he was being bratty and mean to her but it wasn't his fault, sometimes he just had to do something he knew she wouldn't like. He didn't know why he had to. But he did. And then he'd be afraid she wouldn't love him, *couldn't* love him he was such a creep, and even though he guessed he knew she did love him he'd be scared anyway, like somebody was going to take her away too and he wished he had the power to make that not happen but he didn't, there was nothing he or anybody could do about it.

And that would make him mad. So he'd do things to her, say things to her. Mean things. Make believe he was going to punch her or sometimes, even, *really*

133

punch her or be noisy when she was on the telephone or get right up into her face when she was trying to write something or keep on calling her when she was in the shower and could hardly even hear him and had to turn it off all the time.

He did stuff like that a lot. Stuff to annoy her.

He couldn't help it.

I love you. I hate you. He didn't know why he said that. It almost scared him.

He kind of liked this room.

He wasn't aware of liking it or not liking it when he was playing with the guys, but he was now. It was smaller than his room at home and there wasn't much in it. Just a chest of drawers and a table with a chair by it and another small table beside the bed. But he liked the smell. It smelled like wood. Probably because the shop was downstairs under him, or that's what they said.

But it didn't smell perfumy, like his mother's room. It smelled like a guy's room. Like what his father's room probably smelled like.

Who knew?

Who knew anything about his father?

It didn't matter. He was the man now, not his father, and he was lying in a man's room that smelled like wood. When he was older he'd have one just like it. It would be his, but he could invite his mother over. She'd spend a lot of time there, and she'd like being in his room, she'd like the smell. Even if it wasn't perfumy. She'd like it because it was his.

He rolled over. The crickets were loud outside. He was suddenly very tired. On the table by the bed lay the little pile of bones from the treehouse. He looked at them, eyes growing heavy.

The crickets stopped for a long moment and he listened, feeling a little spooky, wondering why they did that sometimes. It was almost as though his heart stopped too.

Then they started up again.

When he was pretty sure they weren't going to do that a second time, he slept.

9:37 P.M.

They moved silently through the field, washed in moonlight, their bodies the pale color of the tall grass, as though the field itself were rising, moving slowly toward the flickering colored lights inside the house.

When they reached the trees they separated, First Stolen to disable the car and telephone wires, Second Stolen to wait naked and bloody in the shadows by the door that led to the kitchen until the Woman signaled to her that it was begun.

The children climbed up into the trees, climbing swiftly, moving quietly as lizards out across the branches that swayed above the deck. Then they, too, waited, watching the people inside through the sliding glass doors.

The people never moved. They sat in chairs watching the flickering colored lights. The man would speak or one of the women would speak. And that was all.

The Woman waited beneath the house by the stilts that pegged it to the hillside until First Stolen joined her a few moments later. He nodded, grinning, his work accomplished.

His teeth had recently been sharpened—the Woman had not noticed when.

The ax he carried was strapped at head and handle to a long leather thong. He slipped his arm through and drew it over his head, slinging the ax across his back, preparing to climb the weathered stilts with her to the deck.

First Stolen and the Woman were too heavy for the limbs of trees.

But the climb was easy.

The Woman looked into the trees and saw that the children were ready. She cupped her hands to her mouth and hissed like a cat. At the door that led to the kitchen she heard Second Stolen crying out as though wounded, whimpering, sounding frightened, heard her beat upon the door, and heard from inside the sounds of sudden movement, the people rising, alarmed, going to the door.

Into her trap.

Above her the children moved farther on the branches, ready to drop.

The Woman and First Stolen began to climb.

9:40 P.M.

Steven finally found the turnoff onto Scrub Point Road the third time he passed it. It was hard as hell reading maps in the dark—he wasn't lying to the hitchhiker about that, he wasn't much good at maps in the first place. All the same he knew he'd overshot it when he wasn't in Dead River anymore, he was in Lubec, and then he turned around and overshot it again and hadn't known he'd screwed up till Trescott.

Anyway, here it was. Puking little sign you could miss in the fucking daylight.

At first the road was macadam but that didn't last long—it turned to dirt in a matter of minutes and he had to go slowly, worrying about how the Mercedes was taking the bumps. There were a lot of bumps.

You paid this much money for a car, you wanted to take care of it.

So it was slow. But Claire wasn't going anywhere. Claire could wait.

He thought about Claire—about screwing Claire, specifically—and felt the beginnings of a hard-on poke around in his tailored pants.

It had been a while.

It was funny how knowing that she'd divorced him made him want her all of a sudden. He hadn't wanted her much the entire year before she threw him out. Of course part of that was the drinking. You'd drink a little and get a hard-on and want some, and then you'd drink some more and it wasn't worth the trouble. You always paid for screwing your own wife anyway. Long ago he'd decided that. A woman thinks she's loved, needed, she takes advantage. It was better to hang out with the boys at the Plaza bar and pick up a stray now and then.

It wasn't that Claire wasn't desirable. Hell, most of the women he did pick up over the years weren't nearly in her class. But they had the advantage of being easy. You could fuck them and then forget it. While Claire came with all her baggage packed and ready. You fucked her one night, you're expected to take care of the kid the next—while she enrolls in some asshole night school or something. And then it's one night a week, and then two. And pretty soon your life isn't yours anymore.

Even Marion was easier, and Marion had made demands of her own. He laughed. He still had some of the scars to prove it.

He remembered Claire's goddamn body, though. A sleek, long-limbed body.

The woman was a racehorse. Tits and ass exactly

the right size—even after Luke was born—and skin so smooth and soft you could just curl up and die.

She wouldn't want to fuck him at first, he knew. She was probably still mad at him. That was all right. She'd come around. She always had. And if she didn't come around he'd fuck her anyway.

Screw the restraining order. What was she going to do? *Call the police on Luke's dad?*

It might even be better if she resisted. He pictured pinning her to the bed, ripping off her clothes, holding her wrists down and sticking it to her. She was strong but he was a whole lot stronger, six foot two and not flabby—the handball saw to that—and he out-weighed the bitch by a hundred pounds.

He could use his teeth on her.

Claire had never liked biting.

His hard-on was serious now and he wondered if he shouldn't have fucked the hitchhiker after all as he cruised the narrow dirt road, his shocks taking a beating, his high-beams on, looking for the house that lay somewhere ahead of him in the gray shades of night.

9:41 P.M.

David was the first one out of his chair but Amy was right behind him, going to the door, the sound of someone in terrible trouble out there—a woman's voice, scared, hurting—and he'd already reached the door and was pulling it open before she remembered that just hours ago the sheriff's office had warned them to hold anyone off at gunpoint if they had to, not just Steven but anybody who was new to them, but by then it was too late, because the shock of the girl's condition wiped away every impulse but the one to help her and get help fast.

She was just a teenage girl.

The door opened and she collapsed across the threshold—or would have if David hadn't grabbed her and held on. Together they helped her inside.

You hardly knew where to touch her.

She looked as though she'd been horsewhipped, beaten for days.

Some of her wounds were scabbing but many more were fresh and deep.

She felt a sudden fear at who or what lay out there in the dark beyond that open door.

She was immediately aware of Claire beside her.

"Claire. The door," she said.

Claire closed it, locked it. "I'll phone the police," she said.

"The number's on a card over the telephone."

"Jesus," said David. He was easing her into a chair.

There were marks on her breasts, her tender inner thighs—everywhere.

"You're all right now," Amy said. "I'll get a blanket for you and a pan and some water and we'll clean you up, all right?"

The girl nodded, gasping for breath as though she'd been running a long way for a long time and couldn't speak.

Amy passed Claire in the kitchen, dialing, reading the card. She hurried past the staircase to her bedroom and pulled the blanket off the foot of the bed.

She checked Melissa in her crib. *Sleeping.* She returned to the study.

"Can you talk? Can you tell me what happened?" David was kneeling, asking her.

The girl just shook her head. She looked like she was about to cry.

"I can't get them," said Claire. Then suddenly her eyes went wide.

"My god," she said. "There's no dial tone."

Amy looked from Claire to David. Their eyes met

and she knew he was frightened too as the girl leaned forward, her pale arms rising.

Embracing him.

Like ripe fruit the children dropped silently from the trees around them as the Woman and First Stolen pulled themselves over the rail to the deck and moved toward the sliding glass doors, watching the people inside—all their attention focused on Second Stolen huddled trembling in the chair and none on the doors, even as the Woman reached out to touch the cool smooth panel of glass and then its metal edge, the door hissing like a blacksnake as she slid it open.

"Mom?"

Luke stood at the top of the stairs, looking somehow thinner and more vulnerable in his pajamas than she'd seen him in years, and Claire suddenly thought, *There's a baby in this house*, though she didn't know why she should think that. She cradled the receiver that she was still holding for some reason and took one step toward him up the stairs, because he had started down.

She didn't want that. She felt some deep insistent knowledge that told her to keep him right where he was.

She heard Amy gasp and David's startled cry, and Luke did too—the sounds stopped him openmouthed on the stairs, and Claire's first thought was for Luke and her second was for the baby who had tugged on her finger this afternoon. She ran to Amy's bedroom and scooped her up, the baby instantly awake, startled and staring up at her, while behind her Amy screamed and things were bumping, breaking, falling, some stop-time wind of destruction swirling at her heels as she ran to Luke and shoved him in his room.

Second Stolen reached for the man and drew herself up, her breasts pressed flat against him. She almost laughed. The man did not know what to do with his hands. They fluttered over her back like frightened birds.

The man was afraid of hurting her. He did not know what to make of her embrace.

She listened for the door, heard it slide open and knew the others were inside.

She felt a wild communion with them compounded of blood and hate, not knowing that in part the hatred was for them—for the whippings, for First Stolen's use of her, for a life stolen which she could never truly miss but which lingered dimly still somewhere far beyond her waking consciousness—and not caring, because this was life now, this hunger, this blood beating in the veins of the man who held her.

She felt rather than saw them enter the room and then heard the man's woman gasp.

She was staring at the sliding doors. At them. At her people.

She pulled him tight to her. And bit down.

At the very last moment the man resisted, pulled away, and instead of the soft flesh of his neck her teeth found only bone but that was all right too, she knew she would have him anyway and bit down harder, grinding her teeth into the collarbone, working her way *into* him, her eyeteeth sinking into the back of the bone, tasting the salt drool of blood and swallowing as he screamed and took her head in his hands, trying to push her, shake her away.

But the man was soft. Not strong.

Her teeth hooked the back of the bone. She pulled.

At the same time she let go, using his weight.

There was a sound like a tree limb snapping as the man fell to the floor, screaming and clutching the splintered halves of bone pressed together pale and bloody glistening wet outside his body.

Second Stolen looked up and saw Eartheater and Rabbit beside her. The others were busy with the woman.

All except First Stolen, who was turning the corner toward the stairs, going for the child. His ax in one hand, claw hammer in the other.

Eartheater and Rabbit were looking at her, waiting. Rabbit was grinning.

She heard the man's woman shriek.

"Mine," she said and bent down over him.

He saw a glimpse of her upside down from the floor, of Amy, his wife, his partner, the flesh he knew so well that it was almost *his* flesh though his own real flesh was screaming now, burning, throbbing so that each new heartbeat was something to live through, to stay conscious through, to get beyond and by, Amy being hauled back into the kitchen by three filthy boys in rags and a ratty-haired girl in some sort of cracked, pale yellow

(impossible)

skin. Amy struggling, screaming, while the woman (their mother? a family? *No.*)

while the woman followed, pointed to the sink with a hunting knife. And the others dragged her forward.

He saw this and in that instant tried to feel his way into Amy's mind, to reach into her and pour out strength and hope to her even though he himself had no strength, the pain had drained it, but to reach out and somehow protect her, armor her with the huge grateful armor of his love. He felt for her, but she wasn't there. She was alone, cut off from him by some terrible black wall of fear.

In the moment before the bright new pain burst like suns before his eyes, he had never felt so lonely.

Amy was in the computer.

The nightmare images played themselves over even as they continued. She was inside the moment and somewhere behind it at the same time, exactly like viewing split screen on the computer, eyes darting back and forth between the old text and the new.

In either place, what she saw was insane.

The girl reaching up to embrace him, something new and cunning on her face as suddenly there was somebody in the

OFFSPRING

*room, seeing them there coming through the door, children,
a woman with a checked shirt and a man carrying an ax,
the children carrying knives and hatchets and hammers and
one of them, the smallest girl, what looked like a garden
trowel and* they were on her now, two twin boys at her
right arm, a boy and girl at her left, dragging her back
to the kitchen sink, strong, so that she struggled hard
and kicked but they dragged her anyway, they pulled
her away from David bleeding on the carpet next to
his desk *and the girl had bitten him, torn him, she saw the
bone crack sharp and bloody up through the skin.*

Pulling her away from him, out of David's sight
lines. So she could not see what they were doing to
him anymore and—

Melissa! Where was Melissa? Where were Claire
and Luke and Melissa and . . . the man with the ax!

*The woman was scarred, horribly scarred, taller than any
woman she had ever known. She was the first one she had
seen* coming at her holding the knife now while she felt
the rim of the sink slam hard against her back, aware
that her robe was open and she was exposed to them
except for the bra and panties, and then there were
cords in the woman's hand, leather cords and she was
tying them to her wrists, a grim almost solemn look on
her face, tying them too tight, cutting deep, hurting
her, the children letting go, the woman turning her
around so that the rim of the sink dug into her belly
and pulling back the cords first left then right and tying them to the hot and cold taps on the sink while the
children jerked her legs out from under her, jamming
the edge of sink into her ribs below her breasts so that
her ribs and bound wrists supported her weight, not

149

her legs, they were spreading her legs and tying them to the legs of the kitchen table behind her and she screamed and screamed, twisting, jerking at the cords, and suddenly there was a rag in her mouth and duct tape shoved roughly over her lips and she couldn't scream, she could hardly even breathe.

She heard pounding from upstairs and knew suddenly where the man with the ax had gone and began to cry. Melissa. Her baby. Claire. Her friend Claire *holding her, Amy sobbing over Danny, her first real boyfriend, in the freshmen dorm in college, her arm soft and strong around her as she sobbed as though her heart would break* and David.

Oh god David.

Don't cry, she thought. *You'll suffocate if you do. You'll die.*

She heard his tortured scream and then more pounding upstairs and a crash of something falling.

The girl was wearing a skin, she had seen that too right away and now she saw what it was.

The skin was human.

She saw the cracked yellow breasts, the darker nipples. As the girl smiled down at her with filthy yellow teeth and placed Amy's bright new aluminum lobster pot in the sink below her, and then adjusted it.

Right beneath her neck.

Even as Claire locked the door behind her she knew it wouldn't hold. She heard David scream, Amy saying no no no and sobbing.

Melissa was crying.

Leading them straight to this room.

Luke stood silent, his face colorless, looking at her. Reading her fear. *What's happening? What do we do?*

"Hold Melissa," she said and thrust her into his arms. The baby stopped crying for a moment and then began again.

She tried not to hear the sounds downstairs.

She tried not to hear or think of Amy.

She went to the window, threw it open and looked down. The bound pile of framing lumber was just below, maybe three feet high by four feet wide. From the window to the pile looked to be a drop of ten feet. Maybe twelve.

She could think of nothing to do but try.

"Mommy . . . ?"

She put her finger to her lips.

She listened. Someone was on the stairs now. Taking his time.

"Luke," she whispered. "There are people in this house. They want to hurt us, and Melissa. We have to go out the window. We have to hide."

He glanced at the window and he was beginning to cry, trying hard to hold it in. The crying was the real thing now.

"Mommy? I'm . . ."

"I know you're scared. It's okay to be scared. But we have to be brave and I'll help you. Don't worry. Put Melissa on the bed and climb up here on the dresser."

She heard the footsteps again. At the top of the stairs.

Close now.

Luke did as he was told. So gentle with the baby she felt a sudden pang of love for him so powerful it hurt.

"Okay, now hang your legs out the window. Sit on the windowsill and give me your arms."

Tears were rolling down his cheeks but he trusted her, he did as she asked and she took his wrists and leaned over the dresser and started to lower him down.

"Mom!" She could hear the panic.

And the footsteps in the hall now.

"I'm going to hold you until you're all the way out the window, do you understand? Then I'm going to let go and it won't be that far because there's a big pile of wood down there and you'll fall on that. You'll be fine. Be a big boy now. When you fall, try to remember to bend your legs a little, okay?"

Luke nodded. His wrists were cold and sweaty.

She reached out across the dresser until her feet were off the floor, her weight sufficient to balance them, inched out farther until she could see over the rim of the windowsill to the pile below and until his legs stopped swaying.

Could she do this? Could he? Could she possibly let him go? For a boy—and not an especially athletic boy— ten feet was a terribly long way down.

She saw him, neck broken, sprawled across the pile.

For a moment she wanted desperately to haul him back in again, bring him back through the window and hold him close and hug him until this all went away and they were together again alone and there was no night and not even Steven to harm them.

152

Melissa was silent.

Downstairs Amy screamed.

Someone was trying the door.

You have to, she thought.

"Bend your knees, Luke," she said, sounding calmer than she had imagined she could possibly sound, so calm it shocked her. *For him.* "I love you and I'll be right behind you. On three, okay? One. Two."

She felt his hands grip her wrists hard once and then relax again.

"Three!"

She willed her fingers open and felt him drop away, and even as the ax splintered the door behind her, watched him plummet down with sudden sickening speed and hit and roll, nearly off the pile but not quite, not quite thank god, just G.I. Joe getting shot again, and then joyfully saw him stand.

She turned for Melissa and this time saw as well as heard the ax come through the door, prying the wood apart enough so that she caught a glimpse of him, a big man naked to the waist and covered with what looked like a layer of grease, grinning, teeth like tiny blackened points, like fangs.

She tore Luke's comforter off the bed and wrapped it around Amy's baby as the ax came through again, the man laughing, watching her through the slit in the door and then suddenly realizing what she was going to do, getting the idea now as she pulled herself up on the dresser and over to the windowsill.

He slashed furiously at the door, stroke after stroke thunder and lightning crackling in her ears as she steadied herself against the upper frame with one hand and clutched Melissa close and pushed off, her back scraping over the frame.

She felt bright quick fire along her spine that was instantly absorbed by the sense of falling, an explosion of absolute freedom so stark and terrifying that her free hand clawed for control, her arm seeking balance as though she were falling through water, not air, and then just as suddenly instinctively returning to Melissa, holding her tight as the impact jolted them and she was on her back, knowing she had got it wrong somehow, and starbursts and night descended upon her all at once along with the scent of spruce and the still, warm air.

David lay numbed with shock staring at the blank computer screen on the desk overhead.

A phrase he recognized—he didn't know from where—kept loping around in his head.

The woods are dark. Are dark.

He was aware of voices on the television and then of someone kicking it in, the smell of acrid electrical smoke almost familiar enough to evoke the memory of who he was and where—and who this surgeon was who operated on him now with naked bloody breasts in his anesthetic dream.

He did not remember her opening his shirt but she must have, to get at what was wrong with him, because now she was tracing a thin red line with her scalpel from his collarbone down across his sternum to his stomach, a thin sound of tearing as she tugged the flesh apart.

154

OFFSPRING

The anesthetic was amazing. His eyes flickered down and he could see his own organs beneath the film of welling blood, his lungs, his heart, and below them his diaphragm, stomach, liver.

Yet there was no pain.

He felt only an itch around his collarbone and a strange cold feeling, like drinking crushed ice in a tall summer drink—so cold you could feel it all the way down inside you.

And it must have been a heart problem, a transplant, because he saw his surgeon reach in slowly and pull the heart free, the heart still beating firmly . . . and in his dream he saw the impossible, saw her raise it to her lips and bite down while her two assistants reached into him too, scrambling with dirty fingers for his liver.

In his anesthetic nightmare he saw her chewing.

His eyes went back to the computer screen—an empty blank—but it wasn't a computer screen now, it was a heart monitor. So incredibly still and lifeless that he knew that he was dead.

"Mommy! Wake up! Mommy!"

Luke was shaking her. She still held Amy's baby.

She'd hit the pile and fallen against the side of the house, hitting her head, and she could not have been dazed for more than a moment because there was Melissa still held tightly in her arms.

She looked up at the window and saw exactly what she had been afraid to see. The man staring down at them. Then suddenly gone.

She got off the pile, grabbed Luke by the arm and started running through the grass.

155

"I know a place!" he said.

Melissa was crying loudly. There wasn't a thing she could do.

"Show me," she said.

The Girl had her knife to the mother of the infant's throat and was going to cut when First Stolen raced downstairs, running for the double glass doors. The Woman stopped him. A questioning, angry look on her face.

He has failed, thought the Girl. First Stolen has failed!

It pleased her.

He pointed toward the doors.

"The child . . . a woman, a boy!"

First Stolen was angry too, and confused. Gesturing wildly with the hammer.

The Woman had not told them there would be any boy, nor any woman other than the one she held here by her curly red hair. Their presence had taken her by surprise.

And that pleased the Girl too. That the Woman could be wrong.

The Woman made a single gesture that encompassed them all—even Second Stolen, Rabbit and Eartheater who were feeding on the kill on the floor.

Go! Follow.

The Girl sheathed her knife and First Stolen was halfway through the doors—then he froze there like a deer paused in flight at the sudden bright lights

156

that swept through the kitchen window, bathing the Girl and the captive woman in light, passing over them and pouring through the rear window to the other room, and they knew that they were no longer alone.

Found it, goddammit! Steven thought as he turned left off Scrub Point Road onto the even narrower dirt road where the mailbox said *Halbard*. He'd been going uphill for a while and now he'd reached the top and was going down over a gentle rise. He could see the house a few hundred yards ahead, lights burning, Claire's and another car in front. He pulled in behind Claire and set the parking brake against the incline.

He turned off the ignition and then the headlights.

The door opened and all he could see was a form in silhouette, followed by other, smaller silhouettes.

His reception committee, coming out to meet him.

What was this, a goddamn cocktail party?

Because they just *kept coming*.

They were moving around the other parked car toward the Mercedes but moving too fast, much too urgently for his liking, approaching him from both sides . . . and it occurred to him that maybe he was actually in some kind of trouble here, that maybe Claire had hired a few thugs to keep him the hell away from her and Luke. It wasn't like her but with a woman you could never know.

It didn't fit though because if these were thugs then half the bastards were midgets. He couldn't put it together. But he didn't like the feel of it either one goddamn bit.

157

He flicked the lock switch on the panel just in case. Then he turned on the headlights again. In time to see the last one running out the door.

Carrying an ax.

And he wasn't any goddamn midget, either.

He reached for the ignition. He doubted he'd ever really been scared in his life, not even seeing Marion's body lying lifeless on the bed, seeing what he'd done to her and wondering what to do next, but he was scared now, adrenaline ripping through him like the Amtrak train to Washington, sphincter twitching dangerously. The Mercedes roared to life and he was set to put her into reverse when he remembered the emergency brake and reached down.

He saw the woman—jesus! she was taller than he was!—reach for the ax and the man hand it over to her at the same time that he felt somebody else climb up on the trunk, the car rocking with the weight, and suddenly there were two explosions front and back that were almost simultaneous, and powdered, slivered glass everywhere, in his hair and on his face and all the hell over him.

He grabbed for the gearshift. Through the glinting white webbing that was all that was left of his windshield he saw the figure of the woman raise the ax again and bring it down with the same terrific force a second time and as he threw it into reverse the windshield collapsed in on him completely. He screamed, hitting the gas so hard that the car shot backward, jolting him, rear bumper grinding against the rocky dirt incline, and the boy—he saw it was a boy now, *some* kind of boy—tumbled off the trunk beside him.

OFFSPRING

Through the completely open windshield he could see the woman, the man and all the rest of them running, coming at him and he just kept shooting backward, hoping to hell there weren't any trees behind him because he couldn't remember and couldn't see a thing through the cracked rear window and couldn't take his eyes off them anyway, these *people* half-naked most of them—women with breasts bobbing as they ran and the boy who was on the trunk getting up with his dick erect, loving this, not a stitch of clothing and not hurt at all like some indestructible ghost or animal and running too. He just kept going, fuck the Mercedes, scraping over rocks, engine whining, realizing he'd been screaming all this time and was still screaming until finally he saw the headlights sweep the crossing onto Scrub Point Road.

He hit the brake, with most of them, the ones he could see, a hundred yards away and not giving up, not by a long shot, coming on fast. He threw the car into drive and felt her skid and tried to straighten her as the man tore out in front of his headlights, throwing something and diving, tumbling over the hood of his car at the same time and disappearing, and he felt the sudden jarring impact against his forehead over his left eye, the heavy claw hammer slashing past him and into the cracked rear window, lodging there headfirst, its handle pointing back to him like an accusatory finger.

The dizziness was worse than any drunk he'd ever been on in his life and he barely missed a stand of white birch that seemed to appear out of nowhere, swerving around them by inches, the palms of his hands bleeding and dusted with glass, sticky where they clutched the wheel.

He felt sick, his stomach rolling.

He felt consciousness bleed away from him through his fingers, sliding down off his forehead and he fought it like he'd never fought before— harder even than Marion had fought *him*—because they were still behind him, not yet far behind him. And the damned black night loomed all around.

10:05 P.M.

They clocked the Mercedes at just under seventy, and though nobody exactly wanted to be bothered with a speeding ticket just then, there were enough hairpin turns along Route 6 so that it was either that or watch this joker kill himself somewhere on up ahead. Plus the car was all over the place, careening around like a wounded buzzard. Plus there was that cracked rear window.

When they got to the flatlands past the closed dark mini-mall where Harmon's General Store used to be, Harrison put on the flasher and siren and they pulled him over.

He stopped so fast they nearly rear-ended him.

Then he got out of the car.

Peters felt his innards freeze when he did that. Because this was how cops got shot all the time, sitting ducks inside their squad cars while somebody blasted away at them through the windshield. Reflexively he hunkered down in the backseat and hoisted the .38. While Harrison and Manetti threw open their doors, got out of the car and drew on him, using the doors as protection. Which was what Peters would have done too if he hadn't been too old and slow and fat.

"Hold it right there!" said Manetti, and unless you could see the twitch in his cheek you wouldn't have known he was scared to hell and back.

"Turn around and place both your hands flat on the roof of your car. Now! Move!"

The guy just stared at them.

And for a moment it got pretty tense there.

Manetti repeated his instructions.

The guy looked bewildered for a second or two and then turned and did what Manetti told him.

Everybody breathed again.

Peters got out of the car. Manetti and Miles Harrison were already walking toward him.

The guy had on a very nice suit but he looked like hell, blood off his forehead wet on the side of his face and staining the expensive shirt. There was some kind of powder all over him, and as soon as Peters got close to him he could see the blood on his hands as well.

Blood on the hands was not the kind of thing you expected from a speeding ticket.

Generally speaking, it was not a good thing.

Manetti held his gun squarely on the man while Harrison patted him down.

They could see what the powder was. The Mercedes had no windshield left at all to speak of.

OFFSPRING

"You want to tell me what happened here, sir?" Manetti asked. But the guy was babbling. Total ragtime.

It was a moment or two before they could figure out what he was babbling *about*, but when they did they got very interested in the guy indeed.

Peters had picked up the spare pint bottle back at the house but he hadn't touched it yet, and now he was sort of glad he hadn't.

"Hold on," Manetti was saying. "You're talking about kids here? Kids and . . . what? A woman?"

"*Some* kind of fucking woman! She took out the whole fucking window!" He pointed to the windshield. "I'm telling you, there was some guy with a fucking ax and . . . god knows how many of them. They were all *over* me! I swear to god half of them were running around naked and they—"

"And you were there for what reason, sir?"

"To see my wife."

"Your wife was there? You can turn around now, sir. It's okay. It's all right."

The guy turned. White as a sheet.

"I didn't see her," he said. "I dunno. I never even got out of the car."

"She lives there?" asked Peters.

"She was visiting . . . people."

"Who? What people?"

"Amy and David . . . what the . . . what the fuck's David's last name! . . . Jesus christ, I can't . . . I mean, I've known them for . . . since . . . ."

Talk about jumpy. Like somebody had shoved a jalapeño up his ass.

163

"Take it easy, sir," said Manetti. "How'd the blood get on your hands?"

"Glass! I've got glass all the hell over me. They took out the fucking window on me! Look at that!"

He spread his hands. There weren't any deep cuts that Peters could see so it must have been mostly powder. It would take some cleaning up. But there were other things that needed to get done first.

The people in that house were in a world of grief.

"Can you remember the name now, sir?"

"Sure. Sure I can. David and Amy . . . jesus . . . shit! *Shit!*"

"What's your name, sir? Your own name."

"Steven. Steven Carey."

And can you remember *their* name now?"

"*I . . .*"

Peters didn't like this. The guy was getting that glazed look in his eyes.

"All right. Can you take us there? Do you remember what road?"

"*I . . . I . . .*"

"It was back this way, right?" Manetti pointed back the way they'd come.

"Yeah. Little dirt road. I can find it I think. But I . . . I don't want to . . . go back there. You know?"

He was almost crying.

"Sir," said Manetti, "your wife and friends might be in a lot of trouble right now. A lot of trouble."

"Yeah," said the man. "Kid, too."

"You've got a child there?"

"Yeah. Son. L-Luke."

164

"I think you should try to take us there, sir. For your wife's and your son's sake."

"Unh-unh."

"I think you should."

"Shit. I'm telling you. I'm telling you. I don't want to go back there. You don't know the kind of . . . bullshit . . . I don't *want* . . ."

The guy was shaking so hard Peters was afraid his knees would give way right then and there. He'd seen people go into shock over a whole lot less. This guy was getting close.

He stepped forward.

"Easy, sir," he said. "Hey. Look. Look at me."

The guy looked. Peters showed him his .38. He talked to him softly, calmly.

"We're all armed. You see? You understand? Plus, we're calling this in immediately, right away. We'll have police in the area before you know it. Nobody's going to hurt you. We'll make absolutely sure of that. We're police and that's what we're for. Okay?"

The guy didn't look too comforted.

"Listen. Did you see any guns? Shotguns? Rifles? Pistols?"

"No."

"Anything like that?"

"No."

"There. You see what I mean?"

"I saw knives. I saw axes. . . ."

"But no guns, right?"

The guy nodded.

"Then you see what I mean? You're safe."

He was wavering.

165

JACK KETCHUM

"Come on, sir. Get in the car. Show us where the road is and we'll go find your son. Come on. We'll get some bandages for those hands too, and for your head, all right? We've got a first-aid kit right here in the car. Okay?"

"I . . ."

"Okay. Good. Come with me."

The guy was definitely hovering close to shock. If he slipped into it all the way they'd never find the place. They'd damn well better hurry. For all Peters knew it might already be too late for these people.

He took the man by the arm and led him to the squad car. He was moving like a sleepwalker.

"In here, sir," Peters said and opened the door. The man got inside. Peters got in next to him.

Harrison and Manetti were set to go.

Peters looked at the man sitting next to him, big and tall and scared.

I hear you, he thought.

They hit the siren and swung the car around, going back.

10:10 P.M.

The naked girl led Amy like a reluctant dog, tugging at the leather thongs that bound her wrists when she hesitated in the darkness.

The path was narrow. Above them was a low natural arbor, a thick canopy. There was little light. It was like walking through a tunnel, a long black twisting tube that shape-shifted under the occasional shafts of moonlight.

Everything was frightening.

A branch brushing her cheek. Another tugging at her robe.

The rush of startled wings in the brush ahead.

Something soft, slippery—the feel of decay under her scraped and bruised bare feet.

The smell of death drifting off their bodies.

They had gone through the field and they were climbing now, a slight incline. Her legs felt unequal to the task. The night was warm but she was shivering, the breeze through her open robe prickling her skin, almost a torture to her.

They moved on and the canopy opened up above them, flooding them with moonlight. They were in a small clearing near the woods. Just ahead the hill became steeper and she could see the black shapes of taller trees outlined against the sky.

She saw her captors too. It was almost worse being able to see them. The dark was almost better.

The naked teenage girl. The two twin boys who ran ahead of her as though this were a game, a pleasure.

What are they going to do to me? she thought. With each step she walked the question seemed to recur afresh, pounding at her like a drumbeat, like a migraine.

What are they going to do?

There was only one other question now and that was for Melissa, and somehow it was impossible to ask herself that without becoming hopelessly scrambled. Melissa was with Claire. Melissa was *not* with Claire. They had found Melissa but not Claire. They had found Claire and Luke only—not Melissa. Any of these but the first, too terrible to contemplate.

Besides, that question could only rarely get through. The pounding continued, the awestruck selfish self screaming for help, searching for a way out.

What are they going to do? *To me.*

Before, as they crossed the field of grass from the house, she had allowed herself—only once—to turn around and look behind her. The tall woman was gone. So was the man, and one or two of the children. She did not know where they had gone and could not even speculate where because of what she did *see.*

168

OFFSPRING

An incredibly dirty boy with a clouded eye.

And the girl with the skin.

The boy carried a pair of arms severed below the shoulder blades. He carried them like firewood.

David's arms.

His wedding ring and wristwatch.

The girl with the skin and the feathers in her hair and the diamond ring that swung back and forth from around her neck carried his legs.

Holding on to his feet. One leg slung over each shoulder.

Ahead of her, the naked teenage girl carried the yellow plastic mop bucket Amy kept in the cabinet beneath the sink. She could not see its contents.

She would not imagine them.

She had almost slipped away just then, she could feel the warm invitation of the cocoon that meant to surround her and protect her, she could feel it sliding gently over her mind—beginning there, sensibly enough, before going on to the rest of her.

But the question had come too, just as automatically, just as unbidden—*What about me? What are they going to do? And what can I do?* They were all one question, and somehow from that time to this the question had come into conflict with the cocoon and defeated it, tearing it away from her until no filament was left at all.

She felt rage so deep in her blood for what they had done to David she barely knew it was there—it was part of her now—and a terrible fear, but mostly she felt the pounding, driving question.

Her mind was clear. Her body knew each moment that she lived through. Saw, heard, smelled everything.

Crickets, pine, the pinprick stars.

She was glad of the clarity, even glad of the hurtful breeze across her legs. It gave the legs awareness. And strength.

Whether it was a good thing or not, whether it would help her survive, did not occur to her. She was her body now.

Her body and her question.

"It's this way, Mom . . . I think. I'm pretty sure."

He knew how uncertain he sounded.

He couldn't help it. It all looked so different at night, even with the moon. And besides, they were running from somebody. He was frightened—and frightened got him confused. And confused got him so mad at himself that he wanted to cry.

But she didn't get exasperated or scold him or anything. She was patient, following right behind.

"It's all right, Luke," she said. "Just keep looking. We'll find it."

He wasn't even sure that the treehouse was a good idea but she seemed to think so—that it might be at least—and that pleased him. There was even some excitement mixed with the frightened feeling because it was like he was the man now, doing things that she was trusting him to do. Doing *something*.

They'd come through the brush and he'd got lucky coming up this time, avoiding most of the stickers, and the only time she'd scolded him was when he stepped on one and hollered and she told him to be quiet—and then, more calmly, said he had to be quiet because they didn't know where the people were or how far back.

There was something in her voice. Something so serious it sort of got to him. So that even if he hadn't realized that she was barefoot too with just her thin dress
on, no more dressed than he was in his pajamas, he
wouldn't have cried out after that for anything.

Though he wanted to. The stickers hurt.

But now there were only mosses and pine needles
underfoot. They were coming up over the top of the
hill where he thought he'd stood that afternoon and
saw the treehouse. He was pretty sure. The treehouse
should have been just up top of the next hill. But he
stood and looked in every direction and then he
looked again and he couldn't see it. No dark platform
anywhere. He couldn't see it and he kept hearing
monsters creeping up over the hill behind him.

"Up here?" she whispered. "Where?"

Melissa made a gurgling sound. What if they heard
her? What if he'd gone over three hills today instead
of just two? *What if he was all screwed up?* He wanted
to cry again.

"Somewhere . . ." He *was* starting to cry. No!

What if he'd come up over the other side?

*There had been a clearing below, to his . . . left . . . just
past the tall grass by the house and the scrubby woods.*

He looked down to his left. He had a clear view. In
the moonlight he could see, and there was nothing
like a clearing down there. Nor directly below, either.

But there! There it was! To his *right!* He'd made a
sort of half circle, because they were running and it
was dark. So instead of coming straight up he'd cir-
cled right—and that was why there weren't so many
sticker bushes up that way.

171

"Over here!" he said.

He ran across the top of the hill and saw it outlined against the sky, higher up somehow than he remembered it—but maybe that was the dark too. The dark was tricky.

"See it?" He pointed. "Come on. Over here!"

"Careful!" she whispered.

But he was already racing down the hill and then up, he could see well enough, and he jumped the stickers and got to the base of the tree and waited for her there, triumphant.

People never look up, Claire thought. *That's what they say. If you want to hide something, hide it up.*

She was betting their lives on a piece of folk wisdom.

But the car keys were in her pocketbook on the kitchen table. There was no getting out of there. There was only hiding.

This is better, anyway, she thought, *than stumbling through the woods at night with an eight-year-old boy and a baby.* She'd have tried the road but they'd have been visible for a quarter of a mile on the road in the moonlight and they'd have had to go around the house in order to get there.

They were in the house, and she wasn't going near it again unless she had to.

The treehouse seemed their best hope.

It had the advantage that you could see the house lights below, over the hills and through the trees. It was far away but you could see them. If anybody came along, any cars, they'd know that and then they could come down again.

172

She was praying for that, and not without reason. Running across the field through the grass she'd seen a car pull in. She'd stopped Luke for a moment in the middle of the field, thinking that this was a rescue. Thinking it almost *had* to be.

Then she heard the car screech down the road again.

Steven? Maybe. He was due.

Whoever it was he had gotten away from them, she was almost certain of that, the car had whined off into the distance, and she could only think that the first thing anyone would do would be to get to the police and get there fast to report this.

"Lie down," she whispered. "Lie right here in the center. I think the platform's wide enough so that nobody can see us from down below. Try not to move much."

Luke did as she asked.

Holding Melissa, who had finally fallen back to sleep again—the night was warm and comfortable, thank god—Claire did the same.

She stared up, blocking out the sounds and pictures that raged through her memory.

Even now, even on this night, the stars were a comfort to her. If she tried—and she *did* try—she could picture children lying out here on truly peaceful nights, away from the adult world, imagining.

She wondered what Luke was thinking, what he was seeing in the stars.

Amy had said that a doctor and his wife had owned the house before them and that they'd had at least two children. The doctor's wife had been living with one of them since her husband died. So the tree-house probably belonged to them. Claire's age now, or older.

She thought of Amy. Heard her screams. She pushed at the sound. Pushed it away.

If worse came to worse they could stay up here till morning, then head out to the road. If the house looked quiet.

Completely quiet.

We're all right, she thought. *We'll be fine.*

The only problem, the only reason her hands wouldn't quite stop shaking was that she felt so isolated here. They *were* so isolated.

Almost . . . trapped.

There was only one way down.

She remembered something and felt a sudden chill.

When she was a girl she had an uncle who owned a dairy farm in upstate New York. Her uncle was a big thick brawny man, well over six feet tall. He had a cruel streak when it came to children and a nasty sense of humor. He was the kind of man who, if you were a girl, would hug you and rub your cheek with his two-day growth of beard until you cried, or if you were a boy he'd want to shake hands with you so he could squeeze your knuckles together, to the same effect.

Claire was nine or ten and her brother Adam about twelve when her uncle proposed a coon hunt one night. Her father was a city boy, bred in Boston. He had never hunted coon and he agreed. Girls, of course, were excluded. But Adam could go.

He'd said later that it sounded exciting—running

through the dark woods after a pack of dogs baying in the distance. And it *was* exciting, he said. Right up to the time the dogs treed the coon and his uncle handed him the .22 rifle and said shoot.

Her brother was a good shot. He had a .22 of his own and practiced at the local rifle range. He looked at the coon about fifteen feet away huddled terrified and exhausted like a big ball of fur stuck immobile where the limb of the tree met the tree trunk—an easy shot for somebody not half as good as Adam was— while the hounds went crazy trying to jump up and pull him out of there, jaws snapping, slobber flying.

Her brother looked at the coon and said no.

His uncle laughed and looked at him and said why? you afraid you can't hit him? and her brother said no, he could hit him all right, anybody could hit him.

His uncle said yeah? in the head? between the eyes? and her brother said yes. He just didn't want to. It was execution, he told her later, not hunting. He had looked to his father for support but he guessed that his father just saw this as some sort of rural rite of passage you just had to go through and his father was having no part of it, taking no sides at all.

His uncle saw that. So he smiled and said tell you what. You go ahead shoot him like you say you can, right between the eyes. Either that or I shoot him in the shoulder and let the dogs have a damn good night of it. He'll fall either way. You choose.

Her brother shot. And never hunted again.

Many years later her uncle died of cancer, died painfully, and she called her brother with the news.

Neither one of them was the least bit sorry.

But she remembered that story now, vivid and terrible as when he told it.

She *felt* it.

She was the raccoon. In the silence of the night she could almost hear the dogs in the distance.

Up here, if they found them, they were helpless.

People don't look up, she thought.

Melissa was sleeping now, but what if she woke and cried?

She felt as though she'd awakened from a drunk to find she'd done something horrible.

That it was stupid, *stupid* to be here.

There was the urgent need to get down at once, on land, where they could run. It was almost physical, a kind of sudden vertigo.

But go down to what? Where was safe? There were supposedly neighbors a mile and a half away or so, but in which direction?

"Mom?" Luke whispered.

She shushed him.

"Mom? *You hear that?"*

And then she did hear it, not far, the sound of a woman crying softly, a woman under exertion. She knew that voice, knew immediately who it was and felt a surge of happiness to know she was still alive, that and a dark fear of what was to come for her and them, linked together like birth and death. She heard soft footfalls too now and someone scuffling through the brush.

She turned to Luke and slid her finger to her lips. He nodded.

They waited.

The sounds seemed to drift like ghosts, taking forever to reach them, freezing her blood as someone giggled and passed to the right of the platform just below her head.

If there was to be any hope for Amy she had to know where they were going, in which direction. She wanted desperately to see.

Yet there was no way she could raise her head. She felt paralyzed—even as the sounds drew slowly away. She was afraid the slightest move might wake Melissa. The slightest waking cooing sound, its echo in the still night air.

She was the raccoon now. Immobile. Sudden death made flesh in the pack below.

It was all she could do to whisper.

"See where they go!" she said.

Luke turned, raised himself slightly on one elbow. She saw his eyes locate them and follow.

When he settled back again his eyes were wide.

"That was *Amy*, Mom," he whispered. "They had Amy!"

"I know," she said. "And it's up to us to keep Melissa safe for her and get help for her as soon as we can."

"Can't we help her *now*?" he said. "They might *hurt* her, Mom."

And she was proud of him—not for his courage because that was just a boy's courage, foolish and immortal. But for his decency, his caring. She realized she was blinking back tears.

"How many did you see?" she said.

He thought about it, counted them out on his fingers.

"Five," he said. "Not counting Amy."

"Was there a man? A big man?"

He shook his head.

"Then we can't go. Oh god! Not yet. He's still around here somewhere."

"But *Mom* . . ."

"We can't, Luke. I love Amy. You know I do. I love her . . . very much. But we can't."

And it will do none of us any good if you start to cry, she thought.

Still she not only knew what the raccoon felt, she finally knew something of what her brother was feeling too and understood his hatred ever after for people who were willing to put you in places like this, places where nothing you do could possibly be right or generous or life giving, and knew she was right never to have mourned her uncle's passing.

10:17 P.M.

"*Halbard*, for godsakes! It's Halbard!"

"That'd be David Halbard," said the cop. "Scrub Point Road. I'll call it in."

The name had come back to him almost as soon as he started thinking about something else.

Thinking about what he was into here, particularly.

They hadn't gotten far. Up until this last bend in the road he could still see his battered car through the rear window.

Maybe it was the sheriff's New York accent that brought his situation home. Or maybe it was the whiskey the fat guy handed him that stopped the shakes long enough for him to think. But here he was with three cops—he assumed the fat guy beside him was a cop, though he didn't look like one. He looked too old, for one thing—and he was carrying scotch whiskey. But he assumed he was.

179

Three cops.

And there *he* was, sitting in the backseat with the old guy. Three fucking policemen.

Shit!

He didn't know which scared him most—going back there or being stuck with three cops doing it.

"Okay," he said. "Look. You know where you're going now, right? How 'bout just letting me off. I really don't want to go back there. Jesus christ, I don't."

The sheriff took his finger off the call button.

"You've had a bad shock, Mr. Carey. We know that. When I call this in I'll call for an ambulance too, get some paramedics out here for you. Believe me, you're a whole lot better off with us."

"Hey, I'm fine now, really. I remembered the name, didn't I? I can walk back to the car and . . ."

"Your car's a mess, Mr. Carey. The only place it's going is the garage. We'll take care of it in the morning."

"I could just wait there, then. I honestly don't want to . . ."

"I appreciate your feelings. But I'm calling this in now. You'll be fine, Mr. Carey, I promise you."

Case closed, thought Steven. Cops. Shit. He felt the old cop's eyes on him. Like he was some sort of freak.

He saw the woman with the ax smashing through the windshield. He saw Marion fat and naked on her bed, her tongue hanging out like a slice of liver, the hairdryer cord sunk deep into her neck.

". . . Halbard place on Scrub Point Road," the sheriff was saying.

"You're where?" said the dispatcher.

"Route Six, just past the mall."

"Closest we got is car twelve-o up at Horse Neck Lane. I'll get them on it."

"Okay. And call everybody else off house-to-house and get them up here. We may have to go looking."

"Will do."

"And get me an ambulance. Lacerations, possible shock. Victim is Mr. Steven Douglas Carey, Connecticut license number M oh nine seven two, one five one eight four, one one three five three. Better make that two ambulances. You don't know what we'll find out here. Over."

"You got it. Over."

He didn't like the cop giving his name. *Why did they have to give his name?* He guessed it was routine. But he was getting a feeling about this. Like the car was shrinking, the front seat pressing up against his knees, the cop beside him subtly closer. It was bullshit. He felt it anyway.

He recognized things along the road now and saw that he'd come in this way, then had driven back blindly, not knowing where the hell he was going, just getting out of there, right along the same route. There was the broken-down tractor parked in the ditch, leaning precariously. And the roadside ad for Jim Beam whiskey. Both of them looking lonely against open empty fields beyond.

They were climbing into the hills. The turnoff onto Scrub Point Road was right around here someplace. Beyond the next bend or two.

Something was wrong. He could feel it.

The squawk box crackled to life.

"Sheriff? Confirmation on that name again?"

181

"Carey. Cable-Apple-Robin-Eve-Yellow. Steven Douglas."

There was a pause on the dispatcher's end, a moment of open air, and he knew before the man spoke again that what he was feeling was far from bullshit, that this was pure trouble, that same white-light edge of something *about to happen* he'd felt back at Marion's, before the cord went around her neck, mere seconds before. Something coiled—cold, frightening, yet almost pleasurable, almost beautiful—inside him. *Easy*, he thought. *Take care. Take stock.*

Winding road. Sixty. Much too fast. Sharp curve ahead. Have to slow down for that. Grassy shoulder. Dropping off down a steep hill. To what?

Nobody around, no lights anywhere.

They haven't locked the door yet.

Wait. Could be nothing.

The cop beside him was looking at him.

The squad car was slowing, going into the curve.

It's not nothing. Go!

"That's what I thought you said," said the dispatcher. "Interesting. We got an all-points on Steven Douglas Carey about an hour ago. Wanted for questioning related to the murder of . . ."

He slammed open the door, felt the cool air rush against him, tumbled and rolled with the impact. He felt stones bruise his ribs and thighs, the wet soft grass, felt the car rush away ahead of him and then heard the squeal of brakes and still he was rolling, rolling down the hill, way down, the grass much higher now, rolling over cattails and tall thick marsh grass that sliced his face and hands yet slowed his fall, rolling finally to a stop in some kind of muck while the car doors slammed overhead. And then he was standing up, dizzy as hell at first, hardly able to stand. He shook his head to clear it and felt mud fly off his face.

He found solid earth again and started running.

The beams of flashlights played over the space behind him, coming down from the top of the hill.

Would they follow?

Marion, you bitch, you told on me. Even dead you told somehow.

He couldn't see anything at first. It didn't matter. He was running through water and then out of it again, not knowing which was which until he got there, just running, slogging through, slipping on rocks, pushing aside the cattails with flailing hands. He smelled stagnant water and rotten vegetation as the water grew deeper and he knew he was in some slow-moving stream, moving gradually uphill against its flow.

That didn't matter either. What mattered was getting the hell away from them and he was doing that, all he had to do was go and keep on going and the months of handball had prepared him, *shit* he was strong, he wasn't even breathing hard and he knew one goddamn thing, that fat bastard wasn't going to be following.

Fuck 'em, he thought. *Fuck 'em.*

Oh you can't catch me. Oh no you can't catch me. If you get too close I'm gone, gone, gone like a cool breeze.

The Blues Project, 1967.

He'd never felt so free.

He heard his own laughter echo through the hills, his feet pounding the clay banks of the stream.

Fuck 'em all.

His eyes were working again, the moonlight bright as the clouds moved away and he saw he was in a forest, deep, with trees all around.

Shit yes, he thought. A forest. Plenty of places to hide.

He pulled off the new silk tie and dropped it in the muck behind him and ran.

10:25 P.M.

Manetti was on the horn again.

"... right. Tell the state boys he bailed out about a hundred yards from Scrub Point Road off Six. Sounds like he's moving upstream. We could hear him laughing down there like a goddamn loon. He keeps on laughing like that he won't be hard to find. Keep me posted."

Peters had his eyes on the rough dirt road ahead, searching for movement beyond the headlights.

He was gratified that Manetti hadn't wanted to waste any time on this character. He'd known cops who would never have been able to take Carey getting away from them. Their egos couldn't manage it. But Manetti had his priorities straight. The people on the hill were priority. And even if he did the murder, this guy was next to nothing tonight.

They pulled into the drive. It looked like half the lights in the house were burning inside.

185

Manetti left the engine running, his headlights and flasher on.

Normal procedure would be to wait for backup but Manetti wasn't having any of that either. From what the dispatcher said backup was still minutes away and minutes could make a difference here.

Peters' hand felt clammy on the butt of his .38. They stepped carefully out of the car.

Harrison threw the beam of his Maglite over the grounds. They saw shattered glass in the driveway from Steven Carey's windshield. Other than that, nothing.

Peters glanced over the house. Saw the steep hill, the stilts supporting the deck around the other side. The house had two floors and maybe a cellar and that was all.

Evidently you walked through this door directly into the kitchen. He flattened himself against the cedar shingle siding, then turned and looked through the window. There was a lobster pot in the sink. Canned goods and silverware scattered on the floor. No movement at all that he could see. He waited, made sure, then nodded to Manetti and Harrison who were poised with guns drawn at the door.

Harrison tried the doorknob. It was unlocked. The knob was turning. He pushed it open and Manetti rushed inside. Harrison swung and covered him and then went in fast beside him. From there he turned a corner into the hall—Peters could see a bedroom and a stairway—while Manetti took the study. Peters was right behind him. The smell of blood telling him just who was going to find what, and where.

He left the door open a crack.

For the ventilation.

The guy lay on the floor near one of the computers. The computer screen and desk were covered with blood. So were the walls and the potbellied stove and the sliding glass doors.

His arms and legs were gone.

You could see inside the guy. His heart was missing and the liver and kidneys were missing, and there was nothing but a wide pool of blood exploding outward from where his genitals had been—as though he'd pissed himself away. Maybe they'd find his dick beneath a table somewhere.

Manetti was staring down at him.

"Fuck this," he said.

Peters knew exactly how he was feeling. How empty and hopeless it is when you're too damn late this time.

"This was a real nice guy," said Manetti. He shook his head. "Fuck this."

Peters gave him a moment.

"Halbard, right?" he asked.

Manetti nodded.

Miles Harrison was coming down the stairs. He turned the corner into the room and went white when he saw what was lying there.

"Anything?" asked Manetti. You could see him pull himself up. He was suddenly all business again. He knew his boys.

Harrison forced his eyes off the body. He swallowed. "Broken door to one of the upstairs bedrooms. There was a kid up there for sure, toys all over the place. Window's wide open, like maybe somebody got out that way, or tried to. The other room's got suitcases, perfumes, women's clothes. There's a bassinet in the downstairs bedroom and a king-sized bed. Men's and women's clothes in the closet."

"Hold it," said Peters. "Bassinet? We're talking about another baby here?"

Harrison just looked at him, thinking, probably, pretty much the same thing he was thinking. That if things could get worse, they just had.

"There's no chance it's been sitting there awhile?"

Manetti's voice was quiet. "They had a daughter, I think it was. A few months ago."

And there was the headache again, pushing from somewhere in the back of his head. Maybe it had been there all along and he'd just become aware of it, just now let it in. He sighed. He thought about the pint in his inside jacket pocket and dismissed the idea. Maybe these people had some aspirin in the bathroom.

"I'll be back," he said.

He was in there with three of them in his hand when he heard a commotion in the den—voices and hurried movement across the floor. Peters stuck his head in.

Manetti and Harrison were at the open door. It looked to Peters like they were about to leave him there.

"Hey? What's up?" he said.

"Screaming," said Harrison. His gun was drawn. "Somebody out there screaming."

*   *   *

188

Claire saw the headlights and the flasher and thought, *Thank god!*

It had seemed like forever they were up there, hoping Melissa would continue sleeping, hoping no one would pass by, hoping for just this—headlights cutting through the night, bringing help and safety and a way out.

Luke saw them too. "All *right!*" he said.

There was no way she could depend on the police to search the woods. Certainly not right away. They might not get to that for hours or even till morning. Meantime these people were still out here.

And Amy was out here too. Not far.

They had to get down.

She'd called her own judgment into question almost constantly these days—inevitable aftershocks of the marriage. Nine years ago she'd embarked on what she thought of as the single *real* adventure that two people could have together—love, commitment, home, and family—embarked upon it because she thought she knew her partner. And had not.

If she could get this wrong, what else? Certainty was like a skittish colt—she couldn't grab the reins.

But Amy was out there. That was certain. And twenty years of friendship left her very little room for doubt for a change.

"Me first," she said.

She wrapped Melissa in the comforter. The baby's eyes flicked open and she smiled. Claire forced a smile back at her. Her foot found the first rung of the ladder. Carefully, she started down.

She glanced up at Luke crouched on the platform. He was watching her protectively, as though ready to reach out and grab her if she missed a step. The breeze billowed her light summer dress.

There was only one board that had felt really loose to her on the way up and she was on it now, edging her foot over so that she was right on top of the double nails for maximum support. Melissa was regarding her seriously, brow furrowed, staring wide-eyed at her chin. She gave the board her weight. It squeaked and held.

She was down. She saw Luke silhouetted against the dark sky, peering over the platform.

"Come on!" she whispered.

He shifted under the railing to the ladder. She glanced right and left down the trail. She felt the insistent need to hurry, an irrational fear that for some reason the police and squad car wouldn't stay, that they'd get to the house and they'd already be gone, leaving them alone in Amy's empty home, still echoing with screams.

Luke dropped down beside her. Her right hand fluttered over his shoulder, across his chest. Needing the contact, needing to reassure itself that he was there, intact, all right.

Then they were moving down the trail together. Clouds across the moon defeated the urge to hurry. The trail was dark and narrow. They passed slowly through the shallow cut between hills and up the other side. Melissa began crying again, swiping with her tiny hands. Claire hugged her close, patting and stroking her back. She subsided.

At the top of the hill they looked across the dark

canopy of scrub and beyond that toward the house, obscured by trees. The sky was brighter there. She could see colored lights—the flasher.

The police. Safety.

They started down.

The clouds passed by and they walked in moonlight for a moment. Then the trees pressed close, leaning meeting at their tops above the trail, blocking out the light.

She stumbled. The path was rocky here. She caught herself immediately but Melissa began to cry in outrage and surprise. She patted her, stroked her, bounced her gently in her weary arms.

And now the trail opened up again. They were in moonlight again, the last stand of trees before the open field just yards away.

"Come on," she said. "Hurry."

Luke tried to edge ahead of her but something made her thrust him back—so abruptly that he almost fell. And she had time to regret this, to feel bad about denying him and pushing him and even to wonder for a moment why she'd done it before the man stepped out into the path, into the light from between the trees.

You son of a bitch, she thought. *Get away.*

It wasn't fair. In her mind she could see the lights and flashers below, imagine the gentle awkward arms of the policeman reaching for Melissa, see them running up the hill, guns drawn, after Amy.

Fear and anger in conflict crawled across her flesh like red and black ants aswarm in battle. She swung at them crazily.

191

Get away.

Fear of him—of his bulk, his excrement smell and his confident stance. Of the eyes like the eyes of dogs gone wild. Of his ax turning slowly in the moonlight.

Anger at his arrogance that he should *dare* to frighten them. A woman, a boy, a baby.

Anger at his cowardice.

Fear of his power.

She wanted to run and attack him at the same time. She knew that neither was right, that neither would get her anywhere, that whichever one she chose would see her dead on the ground in front of him, she saw her body twitching at his feet on that very spot, and knew in an instant that there was only one way she could survive this and that was to do both these things at once, to split herself in two, to run from him and attack at the same time—and that was possible. Because she was not one. She had not been one for many years now.

She was two.

"Luke!"

He was frozen to the spot, staring.

She thrust the baby into his arms. The man stepped forward.

Her eyes scanned the ground. No sticks, nothing to swing to keep him at bay, but the path was still rocky there so she stooped and clawed at the rocks, clawed at them and around them, digging her fingers into the hard-packed soil, but they wouldn't give, they were sunk too deep, the earth would not release its grip.

And he was coming. Swinging the ax.

OFFSPRING

She got down on her hands and knees and clawed, gasping, tears of frustration flowing.

She felt Luke take one step away behind her. Yes. That was right. She turned.

"Run!" she screamed.

Melissa was wailing.

"Mom?"

"*Run!*"

He was almost on them and she was starting to stand so that at least her body would be between them—at least that—when Luke turned and ran and she felt a sudden, release—a sudden sharp intake of breath as though she were running too. She stood up, prepared to meet him, to take the ax deep into her if need be. To hurt him somehow if possible.

But the man only looked at her, a moment of confusion in his eyes. Then he looked after Luke. And she saw who was important to him and what he was going to do.

"*Noooo!*" she screamed, and hurled herself forward, clawing at *him* now and not the unyielding earth. The man flung her aside but she'd thrown him off balance for an instant. He righted himself and she was on him again even as he turned to run, arms around his legs. He made a startled sound and fell, his body thudding to the ground and tumbling away from her, turning, coming up with the handle of the ax. She felt it slam the side of her face, tasted blood. Her grip on his legs weakened but he wasn't free of her, not yet, she was holding on, giving Luke time, even as her vision swam and lights began to burst behind her eyes.

He kicked one leg free and pushed her away, pounded at her face and she swallowed blood this time and felt her back teeth splinter and something bore into her upper palate. She lost her grip. He pulled his leg away. Her hands came off him weak and smeared with mud.

She lay there and saw him stand, searching, looking for Luke. Listening. She struggled to her knees.

Luke was gone. He was nowhere in sight. The trail was an utter miracle of stillness.

Through the pain she felt pleasure, contempt for him, triumph.

They were two now. One of them free.

She felt this even as he reached into her hair, her scream escaping into the silence, and pulled her to her feet.

The Woman crouched hidden amid ferns and brush.

She watched the man coming toward them, plodding upstream.

The man was tiring.

Behind her, deeper back, Eartheater and Rabbit watched, too—Eartheater only sporadically as she peeled the young horsetail shoot, munching on its sweet interior.

The Woman did not recognize the man and his presence in the stream disturbed her. For one thing he was dressed oddly: a coat that did not close over his body but instead flapped back and forth across his chest as he walked, sleeves so short his shirt showed through at the wrists, as though he had taken the coat from someone smaller.

From prey, perhaps.

For another thing, the man was smiling.

It was not the same sort of smile Rabbit wore—and was wearing now—not a fool's exactly. But it had in common with Rabbit's smile a troubling lack of reason. The man was breathing heavily, walking now on the bank and now through the water, his trouser legs thick with mud. He was alone, tired, walking in the night.

Yet the man was unafraid. The man was smiling.

She did not think she had ever seen him before. But the man was comfortable there. He looked like he belonged there.

As her people did.

For a moment she almost feared him.

As he drew closer to her she saw the hardness in the smile, the cold glittering eyes. Saw that he, too, had taken pleasure in the hunt.

Yet compared to her the man was soft.

She had only to watch him breathe.

Instinctively she saw in him a rival for the child's blood. She needed no such rival. The man might have tricks, knowledge. Physical strength was not the only thing. But she watched him with a curiosity she had rarely known. Except for the Cow she had never stolen a man in full manhood, and the Cow was hardly a man, the Cow had never been. She watched him splash through the stream like a child. She was loath to kill him until the smile was gone—until she knew *why* he smiled.

She waited until he passed and then stepped out of the brush behind him into the water, drew her knife and even as he became aware of her and began to turn, slashed through the tendons in back of his left knee.

The man looked at her astonished as he fell, clutching the wound.

He stared at her, eyes glittering and cloudy with pain.

The man would stay there. The man would not get far.

He did not cry out but only lay there in the water, looking up at her in amazement as she waved Rabbit and Eartheater out of their warren.

She gazed at the banks to mark the spot, then moved upstream.

Only once did she look back, and that was just before they started running—when they heard the woman scream.

He had dragged himself up out of the water to the bank, and he was listening too.

She had seen a wolf once whose leg had been broken in a trap. The wolf was pulling, dragging the trap, had torn it from the ground, had dragged it to the top of a hill and stood poised there on three legs panting and howling furiously into the night sky, its jaws snapping.

To her at this moment, man and wolf looked nearly the same.

10:42 P.M.

I'm too damn old for this, Mary, thought Peters. *They were right, they should have damn well left me.*

His heart was beating like a Joe Morello solo, probably in 5/4 time at that, and he couldn't have caught his breath if it sat there half an hour waiting for him. His legs felt shaky and his feet hurt like hell, but he was keeping up, almost, Manetti and Harrison only twenty feet ahead of him, except that they were going *down* the hill while he was just standing on top of the rise, trying not to quit.

He glanced over his shoulder toward the house. They'd called in their position and where they were going but backup still hadn't arrived—he saw no lights but their own.

They'd spread themselves too thin, he realized. And part of that was his fault. They should have concentrated on the immediate area, kept the cars within a couple miles of the Kaltsas home, warning people

197

there instead of going all the hell to Lubec and back. It would have kept them more together. But there was no way to have known that then. No way to know where these sons of bitches would be.

He followed them down, his legs resisting the momentum that might have taken legs younger than his halfway up the second hill before tiring, his own legs scared of the momentum, scared of falling out from under him.

By the time he reached the bottom Manetti and Harrison were halfway up.

By the time *he* was halfway up they were out of sight completely.

He felt like a boat in a trough on a stormy sea—you couldn't make the horizon for the wave action. From here all he could see was treetops. He hauled himself up.

Man against gravity.

At the top his poor legs were shaking so badly his balance was off and he almost tumbled back down again. He stood there a moment puffing, trying to locate them up ahead and when his eyes started to focus there they were, stopped, looking back at him, standing at the edge of a dark stand of scrub pine leaning together treetop to treetop above the path like fingertips meshed in prayer, waiting for him to appear, waiting for the old guy to get in gear and catch up.

And he guessed they saw him step forward a few steps, moving better now over the flat surface of the hilltop, because they gave him a second or two and then when he was about fifteen feet away started into the shadows, thinking that was close enough, they were pretty much together again. And he was coming into the shadows himself, his irises expanding to accommodate the dark, when he heard the first shot and felt something or someone ram him dead on in the stomach, knocking him flat, the .38 spinning out of his hand into the brush, the bottle bursting inside his jacket flooding the night air with the ripe stink of whiskey.

He felt the invasion of steel in his chest and heard Harrison's voice go teenage octaves higher in sharp bright squeals of pain.

The Woman was as surprised as they were.

But she was faster.

Rabbit too, even faster than she was, running past the two men in front of her to the fat man behind and leaping, throwing his body across the man, knocking him down and stabbing with his knife.

She saw this even as she herself reached for the gun hand of the younger, taller man, cracked his wrist and pulled him to her, the gun discharging once, her sharp knife slicing up through trousers, leather belt and shirt to his breastbone in a huge vertical slit that sprayed her body with hot blood while Eartheater hurled herself at the thinner man, her legs around his waist, her left arm over his shoulder as she slashed at his eyes with the three-pronged steel hand spade, the Woman aware—preternaturally aware, like a hawk swooping suddenly through their midst—of all her surroundings as the left eye burst in its socket and the man pressed his gun to Eartheater's neck and fired.

199

The young man in front of her fell to his knees, shocked, clutching at the gurgling spill of white intestines as Eartheater's head slid sideways like a flower on a broken stem, the sound of her flesh like raindrops falling, pattering the leaves of brush and ferns and the trunks of trees. And Rabbit knew too what the man had done because he stabbed the fat man's chest once more and then slid away, ran to where the thin man flung his sister's clutching body off him, and leaped upon his back. Eartheater's body turned, falling. Rabbit stabbed.

The man fired into the trees as the Woman jumped and kicked him in the chest, whirled, stabbed him once through the neck, his windpipe cracking, withdrew the knife as Rabbit dropped off him and the man leaned forward to clutch his neck, his gun dropping away, and then took the knife in both her hands, turning the blade toward her, and stabbed him again through the back of the neck this time, shoving the knife deep, grinding up past the cervical vertebrae of the neck into the brain.

The man trembled wildly, his mouth spewing fountains of dark arterial blood. Then fell.

The night was silent.

The blood across her face and breasts began to dry.

For once, Rabbit was not smiling.

The Woman gathered up their weapons, their guns.

She could not find the fat man's gun. She supposed it had fallen in the brush somewhere out of sight.

She stood for a moment beside his body. She looked at him closely. Somehow he seemed familiar to her. A face glimpsed long ago. But the Woman could not remember.

His jacket was soaked through where Rabbit had used the knife. She kicked him in the ribs for good measure. The fat man did not move.

She looked again.

The man was a mystery. His familiarity to her.

But there were other mysteries.

The infant child was one.

She had heard the woman's screams not far from this place and hoped that First Stolen had found them, all of them, the boy, the woman—but mostly the infant spirit who would remove the taint of un-spilled blood.

There had been no further screams.

There was nothing to do now except go and see.

She hauled the body of Eartheater up onto her shoulder. The Woman did not look at the gaping wound. It was not a good thing to dwell on how an-other died.

With Rabbit silent behind her and Eartheater's still-warm blood trickling down across her back to the earth that named her, she turned toward the sea.

Luke hid behind the tree in the dark shadow of the treehouse platform above him, looking back down the trail. At the man and his mother.

He could see them clearly.

The man had one hand twisted in his mother's hair, dragging her behind him at first—she was crying, try-ing to walk backward, stumbling—then thrusting her

201

out in front of him, the head of his ax pressed flat into her lower back.

A warning.

The man would tug at her hair and the ax would dig into her back and make her gasp in pain.

He was enjoying hurting his mother.

Luke had never been so scared, watching the man hurting her.

He remembered something he'd forgotten for a very long time. He'd come downstairs one night awakened by loud voices and saw his mother backed up against the refrigerator, his father with one hand around her neck and holding a glass of something with the other. His father would alternately drink from the glass and hold it up to her face as though he were going to hit her with it maybe, and all the time he was yelling that she had no business telling him what to do with his time, that he'd be home when he fucking wanted to *if* he fucking wanted to and she could just go fuck herself and wait for him or not as she fucking pleased.

He'd used the F word a lot and he was saying it in a mean way, not the kind of joking way the kids used it in the playground at school, and all the time he had her by the neck she was telling him to let go, please let go Steven—trying not to cry, he could tell. But Luke was crying, though he was hardly even aware of it, and they heard him and when his father turned and saw him he did let go finally, and his mother went over to him and brought him upstairs.

The next night she had wanted to talk.

He hadn't.

It was weird but he wished he had now.

Now that he was so scared for her again.

Melissa was making crying sounds and that scared him too. Not loud, but the man was going to hear them if he didn't do something.

He didn't know what to do.

They were getting closer.

His mother had told him that you had to be real careful with babies, that when they were little like this you could hurt them by mistake without trying. If Melissa had been a kid his age he would have just put his hand over her mouth to shut her up . . . but what if he did that with Melissa and it hurt her?

Oh, jeez, they were close!

His mother was making gasping crying sounds from the man pulling her hair and shoving her and he guessed that was mostly what the man was hearing but *they were too close and he* had *to do something with Melissa.* He looked down at her and she looked so small almost like a puppy and he was afraid to hurt her and afraid to keep his hand *off* her because the man was going to hear them and find them and drag them too. There were tears running down his cheeks but he put his hand over her mouth because he *had* to he couldn't help it and the sounds almost grew louder for a moment—he guessed Melissa must have realized what he was doing and started crying seriously, squirming and pushing at him as he thought, *Please, Melissa, I'm sorry, I'm sorry, only just for a minute, please,* and he increased the pressure because she was still too loud, afraid of hurting her all the while and feeling that he had to go to the bathroom bad and watching the man and his mother abreast of them now, passing, his mother's voice shrill and thin as the man yanked at her hair and she almost fell, then moaning as they passed, her voice and their scuffling feet along the trail masking Melissa's crying sounds—and knew that she had saved him a second time.

He hardly dared breathe himself.

He kept his hand there on her until they were over the rise, easing off on the pressure and easing his hand off her slowly, as gently as he could. Finally he took his hand away completely. And when she wasn't hurt or dead, when all she did was look at him he raised her up and kissed her on the forehead a dozen times. He loved her as much as he'd ever loved anybody in his life right then.

She looked at him strangely, as though wondering what this new game was supposed to be. And then smiled.

And suddenly he felt the pull.

She was getting away from him. *His mother.*

She was going out of sight, over the rise.

She'd be gone.

Suddenly he was terrified—that if he didn't follow he'd just never see her again. He *knew* he'd never see her.

It was as certain to him as the fact that he was in the third grade and that his mother thought his room was always messy and that he had a bike and a skateboard back at home in the yard.

He wouldn't see her! He'd lose her!

Mom!

It was a pull so strong he shook in the wake of it.

He was terrified of the man. The man was *horrible.* Worse than Jason, worse than Freddy Krueger— worse than *anybody.*

But if his mother went away he'd be . . .

. . . *alone.*

His heart thumped harder now than when the man had passed, he was *that scared,* a raw panic that clogged his throat and he had to do something *now,* do something fast, he couldn't wait for help because he couldn't even *see* the man and his mother any- more, and help was all the way down there minutes and far away—and maybe the police were even gone already, disappeared, they *could* be. He had to follow and find them. Had to see her, know she was there nearby and keep her in sight.

He almost started out across the path. And then he thought, *Melissa.*

How could he take Melissa?

Melissa would cry!

Her diaper would get wet or something and she'd cry!

He felt a moment of total confusion, almost cursed his mother for leaving this baby there with him . . . and then a kind of instant clarity that made him feel suddenly older, a whole lot smarter than he'd ever thought he was and maybe even *up* to this, *ready* for this, up to following and not getting caught and maybe even helping somehow.

Helping her.

He climbed the ladder again.

He lay Melissa down in the center of the platform,

bunched up one end of the comforter to form a kind of pillow and wrapped the rest around her, tucking it tight so she wouldn't catch cold—though the night was still pretty warm.

"I'll be back," he whispered. Melissa made a hiccupping kind of sound and flexed her fingers, reaching out to him.

"Don't you worry."

He climbed down and sprinted to the top of the hill.

He felt a huge weight lift away as he saw them below, moving slowly through the clearing.

The man was still pushing her, hurting her, but there she was, walking, standing, still alive.

Staying in the scrub, in the shadows and only just close enough to keep them in sight, his lifeline still strung tight between them, he followed.

A little later he heard gunfire in the hills.

It sounded like firecrackers. But Luke knew it was guns.

It might be help and it might not. He hoped it was. But it was far away by then and not his problem.

His problem was to keep her somehow. To hold on to her. And by doing so, make them back into a family again.

To that end he aged—and grew stealthy in the moonlight.

11:15 P.M.

Somewhere a baby was crying.

It was dark in the cave and she couldn't see beyond the dim glow of the banked fire. She heard moans and the rattle of chains and the baby crying and for a moment thought, *Melissa?* but the voice didn't belong to her.

She knew her baby's voice.

The girl pulled her inside and handed over the leather thongs that bound her to someone else, she couldn't see who at first, and then a figure appeared before the fire, piling on first twigs and then sticks and logs, and as the fire rose up she saw that it was one of the twin boys at the fire and the other who held the thongs.

She heard the girl drop the plastic mop bucket to the ground. The fire spread, light and shadow licking the walls of the cave, and she could see them now, the teenage girl covering her scarred and wounded nakedness with a man's faded blue shirt that was much too big for her, pulled from a pile over three feet high that lay near the entrance. A mouse, startled, ran from somewhere within the pile into the shadows.

She looked around the cave and felt reality dart away, too. Into the shadows, like the mouse.

The walls were hung with skins.

Some she could identify. Raccoon, skunk, deerskin.

Others were unfamiliar. Pale and translucent.

She refused them and looked away.

She saw a rough order. Except for the clothing and a pile of tools and weapons their possessions were arranged according to size, not function.

Small cooking pots, empty tin cans and full ones, a small broken wicker basket, tarnished brass candlesticks and a dirty stuffed teddy bear were all thrown together. Smaller things—spoons, forks, spools of thread, keys and key chains, pairs of broken eyeglasses, wallets, coins, a corkscrew, and a cane chair from a dollhouse—formed a pile directly at her feet.

Another pile rose halfway up the wall, a jumble of larger items. A pair of dented lobster pots side by side with an antique pine milking-stool, its legs corroded and caked with dirt, marked white by salt water. These beside a faded wooden checkerboard, a plastic five-gallon bleach container, and an empty screened cat carrier. These on top of a ghetto blaster—smashed—a suitcase, and a dented metal tub.

There were piles of bleached white bones all along the walls of the cave.

Jawbones. Skulls.

Animal and . . . otherwise.

OFFSPRING

She saw the boy with the clouded eye and the girl
who wore the skin of breasts skewering wrists and
ankles with rusted meat hooks tied by loops pegged
to the roof of the cave. Legs and arms dangling, ooz-
ing viscous blood. Swaying.

Not David's anymore.

To think of them as his was to open a door that
needed to remain tightly shut, a door within and beyond the cave that opened up to pure blank light and
emptiness.

The baby cried.

She saw it now, lying on a pile of pine needles and
branches over which had been tossed a single stained
blanket with frayed edges. No older than Melissa.

Naked. A girl.

She smelled it too. A thin trail of feces glistened between her open legs.

The others ignored her.

The baby was hungry. She could feel her breasts
ache in automatic response.

*She had only this week begun to steer Melissa toward
solid foods, starting with just the tiniest taste of Beech Nut
rice mixed with formula.*

She still had plenty of milk.

Soon her breasts would be leaking—that was automatic too. She felt a flash of frustrated rage. For her
body to do that to her now would be a complete betrayal of itself. Of her.

Of that part of her that was not the body. *Infuriating.*

She would not allow it.

She looked away.

Because it ought to have been Melissa she was with, her

209

own child in her own home, at her breast in her bedroom. Not this . . . creature . . . who at three months old was already as filthy as the rest of them, thin foul liquid dribbling from between her legs.

She did not want to think about the baby. It was only there as another torment to her, to squeeze the tears from her eyes, to make her weak.

She would not be weak.

It's dead, she thought. *I just killed it.*

To hell with this baby.

They were beside her now, both the twins, pushing her past the fire, deeper into the cave. She let herself be pushed. There was no use trying to resist them. Not with her hands tied. She had seen the strength of the teenage girl . . .

. . . seen it as she pulled David down, her arms curling round him like snakes, her mouth open . . .

She heard metal rattle on metal again. She saw the man chained in the shadows in the back of the cave, saw him leaning forward against his chains, his body thin and slack and so pale that even the firelight's orange-red glow failed to lend him color, his eyes empty, unseeing, looking *through* her as she passed and they shoved her forward and then turned her beside him a few feet away and pushed her back roughly to the wall.

The man did not seem to register that she was there. His gaunt jaw hung open and flies buzzed in and out, settling on his teeth and tongue.

She saw the reason for the flies immediately.

A puddle of urine at his feet, a pile of feces between his legs, tumbling out from behind and beneath him.

210

She realized the man had been there for many days. Standing amid his own excrement.

She felt her stomach heave.

Already the swarm had found her, buzzing across her arms and face.

She swiped at them, the twin boys laughing at the awkwardness of her bound hands.

The girl stepped toward her past the fire. The boys made way.

The girl stood in front of her and untied the thong on her left wrist, then pushed both arms behind her and tied her again, tight.

She smiled and ran her fingers through Amy's long brown hair, pulling roughly through the tangles, through the burrs and twigs. Her eyes flickered up and down her body.

She was aware again of her open nightgown, of the flimsy bra and panties. The girl's eyes pawed her.

The girl turned and walked back past the fire. A moment later she returned carrying a length of clothesline and a knife.

And it was not the knife she was suddenly afraid of, it was the line, because the girl was all business with the knife, looping about fifteen feet off the line and cutting it, dropping the knife nearly into the urine pooling out beside her and throwing the line over a wide outcropping of rock above her head.

She watched the line sway and dangle—then saw the girl pull it tight to neck level and panic seized her and she began to struggle. But the twin boys had moved in close beside her, they had her arms now and they had knives too and placed them on either side of

211

her ribs and held them there sharp and cold against her
flesh, not cutting her, barely pressing in. But enough.

"Please," she said.

She looked at the girl. The girl was concentrating,
making a knot in the line. Deaf to her.

The girl made several tries before she got it right, a
loop at the far end.

*Small, she thought. Not nearly large enough. Not to go
over my head.*

So they were not going to kill her after all. Not yet.

The girl pulled at the cord. The knot slipped forward.

She reached abruptly into Amy's hair again and
pulled it back so tight that she cried out, gathered it into
a fist and then slipped the loop around it, pulled hard
on the cord and then let go with her hand. Where her
hand had been the cord now bound her hair together.

She felt a thousand pinprick stabs of pain all along
her hairline and through her scalp, yet she could bear
this, it was better than hanging, better than dying
never seeing Melissa again in this place with flies
crawling over her eyes and into her nostrils, the baby
squalling, wanting, *smelling* the milk inside her. She
could bear this. And live.

She knew she could live.

*Until the girl reached down for the other end of the rope
and pulled, the twins helping, her feet suddenly lifting off
the cool floor of the cave so that she dangled in midair and
each of the pinprick stabs multiplied a thousandfold, burning, her body swaying and her mouth falling open in a
choked-off, guttural scream.*

The flies flew in and out.

11:47 P.M.

At the place where the trail branched off to the cliffs the Woman handed Eartheater's body over to Rabbit, placing it squarely on his shoulder, its ruined neck belching a single spurt of blood and fluid across the moss and lichen.

She watched him until he was out of sight, moving toward the cave.

He handled his burden well.

He would grow to be strong—as strong as First Stolen. If only someday he would develop sense.

She had seen no sign of First Stolen, nor of the screaming woman, the boy, or the child. So that it was best now for all of them to return to the cave. To regroup if First Stolen had not found them, and reconsider.

It was early. The moon was bright. There was still plenty of time for the hunt.

She turned down the hill toward the stream, making her way carefully through the deep woods to the place she had left the man hamstrung, bleeding in the water.

He hadn't gotten far.

She saw him on the bank, turned over on his side, both shoes resting beside him, trying to bind the wound with his long black stocking. But his hands were trembling with the pain and kept slipping—he seemed to have no strength in them. He couldn't get it tight. Beneath the dried brown blood his face was pale. His eyes burned as she approached him.

"Get the fuck away from me."

The man was dangerous.

Fascinating.

A wolf in his trap.

"You fucking crazy bitch. Get the . . ."

She drew her knife. She knelt beside him and placed its point to the bridge of his nose directly between his eyes. She waited until the sharp point of the knife had its say in him, until the fire burned low in his eyes and he grew calm with respect for what she could do to him now or any time.

She put the taped handle of the knife between her teeth and took one end of his stocking in either hand and pulled it tight, knotting it twice.

The man's breath hissed through clenched teeth. Except for that he made no sound.

She stood and slid the knife into its sheath. The man looked up at her, his dark eyes narrowing. She saw him glance at the guns pushed through her belt.

She smiled. This wolf would bite if given the opportunity.

She offered him her hand.

She would tame the wolf. If it could not be tamed then she would kill it. But first she would see.

She stood in full moonlight and watched the man's eyes drift across her scarred face to the fierce lightning streak through her hair. She knew the eyes were afraid of her and that was good. She knew too that they dreamed and planned, and that was not so good.

His eyes were thin narrow slits. They glittered in the moonlight. Behind them, in pain, hid the wolf.

She would draw the wolf out, snapping.

He took her hand.

She lifted him to his feet and draped his arm over her shoulder. The man did not look at her again, only at the earth below, careful of his step as she moved him easily through the woods up the hill to the path, then over the path where Rabbit had come before her, to the cliff and the seawall.

Bringing him to his lair. And to his cage.

11:55 P.M.

Luke kept to the rocks, well behind them, as they walked the beach.

In the tide pools beside him seaweed like the black legs of spiders waved and swayed from barnacle-encrusted boulders. The rocks were splattered with white guano and the broken carcasses of land crabs.

He watched his footing—and he watched them. Two dark shapes leaving footprints in the lunar sand.

It was no longer possible for him to hear his mother. Maybe the man had stopped hurting her so she didn't have to cry out anymore, or maybe it was just the distance and the tide churning through the narrow channel that lay between them. Maybe she was still crying. He heard the roar of waves. That was all.

He had no plan. He had no idea what he was supposed to do or when. It just seemed right to follow, not letting the man know he was there. He wondered how long it was till daylight. Someone might come along then. But he thought that daylight was probably a long way away and he had no idea what he would do till then. Just keep following them, he guessed. They might keep walking forever, right into daylight. It was possible.

The man was pulling her along by the front of her dress, making her keep up with him. The man walked fast and his mother stumbled sometimes but the man wouldn't stop, just pulled at her until she got to her feet again and started walking.

It was hard keeping up with them.

He was tired and sore and his feet hurt from the barnacles and shells on the rocks. But it was better near the shoreline, faster on the wet sand, and the rocks were there to hide him.

The air was damp here, chilly from the salt spray. He was thirsty.

From here the rocks angled out farther past the tide line. It was the first time he'd come across the problem. He had to stop a moment to consider it. Either he'd have to risk walking the open sand for a while— *the man could turn and see him*—or else he'd have to stay with the rocks. And he couldn't think for long because they were getting ahead of him, he was already far away.

The rocks or the man.

The rocks felt safer.

He went over them on all fours. They were slippery. Waves rolled in and filled the tide pools, each wave bigger than the next until his pajamas were soaked and his hair was dripping. He had to step into the tide pools too and that was hard because you couldn't see how deep they were or what was in them—crabs or eels or what—hidden beneath the shifting foam.

He pulled himself up onto a low flat slab of granite. It felt slimy under his feet.

Something growing there.

He hopped over to a rounder, higher rock. His footing there was better. He crouched and went hands first onto an even bigger one, its surface sparkling with mica, crawling over it sideways—and then he was going to have to jump, because the rocks were angling back to shore now all except for this last one. This last one formed a kind of point. It was long and flat but half-hidden by the water, a couple feet away.

He went into a crouch again and took a breath and jumped.

He hit the rock and his legs almost went out from under him, he had to scramble to keep his balance, but he got there, he was standing, and he looked up to see how far they'd gotten because he knew this had taken him longer than it should have, he should have risked the open sand, and he saw them way down the beach so far away that even if the man turned Luke doubted he'd notice him now standing way back here, and he started for the next rock which was an easy one going back toward shore when the wave slammed into his legs and knocked him over.

The backwash pulled him off the rock and under. He swallowed water. His feet touched sand and then it was gone again, he was rising. Then going under. He felt the undertow grip him like the invisible pincers of a huge crab, dragging him back until his lungs were throbbing.

He rose again, broke surface and opened his eyes and wiped away the sting, gulping air, coughing. All he could see was another wave coming toward him, rising, and beyond that, another wave and beyond that, moonlight on the water. *Where was he? How far out?* He turned, splashing, trying to get his bearings as the wave caught him and pulled him forward in a rush of white water and he saw he was headed for the rocks, dark, gleaming, racing toward him like sharks, and something told him to go under.

He took a breath and ducked his head, threw his arms out in front of him and rode the churning water, felt himself turning upside down and back again, felt as though a roller coaster were taking him and tried to straighten as his forearm slammed against stone and went instantly dead and burning and the wave drove him into the sand, piling him in hard, scraping deep across his chin and chest. He rose almost to the surface, the breath bursting out of him past his lips as something hit him in the belly and the wave dragged him across the blunt narrow edge of a second rock.

His body folded in on itself. The sand swirled over him.

He turned face up.

Salt spray hit his cheeks.

His head, then his back drifted up to the sand at the shoreline.

He felt himself settle in, the sand washing away in tiny trenches around him, outlining his body. He lay there a moment gasping, the waves lapping gently now at his legs and rising up over him, lifting his arms spread wide at his sides, trying in vain to float him back again.

He had no idea where he was.

His left arm throbbed. His chin, chest and stomach burned in the cool breeze.

There was only one thought in his mind—that he'd lost them. Not that he'd almost died. That he would turn and not see her there, that somehow between then when he was standing on the rock and now his mother would be gone, disappeared.

He raised himself up on one arm, resisting the urge to cry, the *need* to cry, and looked behind him up the beach.

He was closer to them now than he'd ever been.

So incredibly close it was frightening.

He could see them clearly, his mother's dress torn in front where the man had been dragging her, her hair shining in the moonlight, even her face wet and stained with dirt and tears as they turned away from him toward the high jagged cliffs.

He flattened himself against the sand, motionless as driftwood, and watched them start to climb.

PART V

MAY 13, 1992
NIGHT

12:00 MIDNIGHT

Claire entered the cave to their silent stares, to the crackle of the fire, to the pounding waves far below, and to Amy's low moan.

The man had thrust her inside and stood behind her blocking the narrow entrance. As though worried she would run. As though she *could* have run seeing Amy there.

And what they'd done to her.

Her hands flew to her face, palms pressed deep into the sockets of her eyes. She shook her head against the sudden onset of dizziness and nausea.

It passed.

Her hands dropped to her sides, clenched into fists. She took a breath. She looked.

Before he retired, her father had been a high school teacher in Brookline, Massachusetts, an English teacher, who always seemed to like the movies—*films*, he called them respectfully—easily

225

as much as he liked Jane Austen or Proust (though perhaps not quite so much as Hardy, Joyce, or Henry Miller), and he had directed her to and even taken her to films through much of the late 1960s and early 1970s, when bold, often bleak personal visions were still very much in vogue, when American audiences, educated and troubled, apparently would still rather pay to see movies rooted to home truths about their lives than escapist melodramas and comedies.

Bonnie and Clyde. Easy Rider. Sunday Bloody Sunday. The Wild Bunch. Medium Cool. The Graduate. Five Easy Pieces.

Her father loved some of these movies until the day he died. She had loved them too.

Though her father had been a gentle man these films were often as bloody as the Vietnam War or the Chicago riots which in many cases formed their metaphorical and certainly their historical backdrops. Her father liked to quote the director Akira Kurosawa on the subject.

"To be an artist," said Kurosawa, "means never to avert one's eyes."

Her father was no artist, though he did paint the occasional muddy watercolor on a Sunday afternoon. Nor was Claire. But it was the second part of the statement that stayed with her through the years, the wisdom in the notion of not averting one's eyes. She had done exactly the opposite with Steven, had looked away, ignored his drinking, ignored what she knew to be true, and since had flogged herself for it a thousand times.

OFFSPRING

The statement counseled toughness, honesty, rigor—
and she did not so much remember it now as know
that somewhere deep inside her, her father's exacti-
tude of spirit moved in her, informed her, destroyed
at first impulse that urge to retreat from what she saw
that already wished to content her with mourning
her friend's fate and her own and blur her sight.

"Let her down," she said.

Her voice was never very loud—not unless she was
yelling at Luke—and it wasn't now. But it sounded
loud in the cave. More firm, too, than she would have
anticipated. Almost a teacher's voice. Almost like her
father's.

Claire shook, trembling. The voice didn't.

No one moved except two of the children—twin
boys—who gazed at one another in surprise and
then sniggered. Behind her the man laughed too, his
voice pitched higher than she'd expected from a man
his size. Almost a giggle. *Idiotic*, she thought. Evil and
idiotic.

"Let her *down*."

She saw the teenage girl, the one they had let into
the house, her torn body covered by an old blue shirt,
bent over a yellow plastic bucket, transferring something from the bucket to a rusted cast-iron pot. There
was water in the pot.

The girl had her back to her, had turned when
Claire entered and turned again now when she
spoke, but only smiled and tossed her hair and returned to what she was doing.

At the back of the cave Amy groaned and tried to
swallow.

227

Even that small motion caused her to sway, and the swaying caused her to moan.

They had cut away her bra and panties. Her robe hung open, dangling off her shoulders.

Thin rivulets of blood trickled down from her hairline across her face and neck, over the tops of her breasts, staining her robe at the collar.

Dozens of them.

Her body slowly turned.

Flies buzzed all around her.

The naked man beside her shifted too, trembling, rattling his chains. There was a girl wearing some sort of skin strapped together behind her back standing in front of him, tugging at the raw flesh of his penis, totally involved with that and ignoring Claire completely.

Claire hesitated, picturing Luke and Melissa huddled in the darkening woods. And then stepped forward.

No one stopped her.

She walked past the twin boys to the girl and even as she became aware of what the girl was doing, of the bone piercing the chained man's scrotum, plucked the knife from the back of her belt.

The girl whirled, snarling—but Claire was all clean motion, reaching up and severing the clothesline and reaching down for Amy in a single sweep of her arms, cutting through the lines that bound her wrists.

Amy screamed and gasped in release and then Claire was holding her, her warm familiar body, barely able to stand at first, Claire clutching her to make her stand as the girl plucked the knife roughly from her hand and held it first to her throat and then to Amy's—and suddenly the cave seemed to close around her. The man, the teenage girl, the boys, all of them appearing so fast and tight around her she could barely breathe with the stink of their bodies and their breath pouring over her like the heated breath of dogs. The man shoved her back against the wall. She clung to Amy's robe, protecting her with her arm, keeping the connection, and felt the arm go numb as her elbow struck granite.

She tried to ignore it. To ignore them all.

The flies swarmed angrily.

Amy looked up at her. She touched the bloody hairline. There was a film of pink in her eyes, a thin pink film of blood. Claire wiped them with the sleeve of her dress, wiped her friend's face and lips and closed the robe over her body.

The man stepped forward and reached into her hair. This time she resisted.

"No," she said.

But the man wasn't really trying. He was laughing at her.

They all were laughing. Moving back, easing the circle, giving him room.

The man shifted his hand to the front of her head and bumped it back against the wall, not hard enough to do her any harm but hard enough to hurt, bumped it over and over in measured cadences, the pain nothing at first and then cumulative, playing with her, until lights started flashing behind her eyes. She held tight to Amy and waited, waiting out the hurt, Amy her lifeline and Claire hers, listening to

their laughter and somewhere, to a baby waking, crying, its voice harsh and echoing through the cave.

She gritted her teeth and waited.

Thump.

And slowly felt something start to build in her,
something she knew was dangerous to them both
and barely under control but irresistible as they
laughed and the infant howled and one twin boy
reached out with one hand to pinch and twist her
nipple and the other to poke her ribs.

Thump.

Laughter.

Her stomach. Her ribs again. Poking.

Bullies. Like Steven. Like all of them.

Thump.

Then a pair of hands reached across her to Amy's
shoulders, trying to pull her away—the hands of the
girl who had deceived them.

Claire clung tight, felt Amy's cool fingers clutch her
arms, the pressure inside her building, knowing that
it was only a matter of moments now and they would
separate them again, this possibly for the last time,
possibly forever, that the girl was far stronger than
she and could do that, not being able to bear that in
any way whatsoever and aware of Amy sobbing and
the sense of danger and anger and awful potential
mounting until—

Thump.

Something ripped bursting inside her and she
pushed back off the wall in fury and put all of her
weight into the forward thrust of her knee, the sound
of it loud as an ax chopping into him or into the trunk

of a tree until he screamed full into the echo of the sound, drowning it, clutching at his groin and falling to his knees in front of her and rolled toward the fire, stopping just in front of the fire, rolling as though *on* fire, the fire licking at his balls, at his idiot brutal manhood.

And as the teenage girl jerked Amy out of her arms and the twins and the girl with the skin grabbed Claire and threw her to the ground, as they kicked her in the ribs, in the head, in the back, as the pain raced through her and off her like a bird of prey skimming the ocean, she watched the man rolling by the fire.

She watched and watched.

12:05 A.M.

Peters' chest felt like a breeding ground for killer bees.

It was the whiskey. It stung like a sonovabitch in the two shallow knife wounds near his sternum.

But it was also the whiskey that had saved his life.

Supposing he was going to live.

Forget that he smelled like the floor of the Caribou the day after New Year's Eve. He *looked* like a stuck pig. The stain went from his armpits to his belt buckle, all the way down his sides. In the dark it would be indistinguishable from blood.

They'd have taken one look and thought, that's one dead drunk lying there.

There was blood all right but he wasn't bleeding to death. Not yet. The kid had been in a hurry, though from the feel of it he suspected his knife had chipped a bone. The wound in his side was much deeper and there was more blood there than was running out of his chest but the kid had cut into gristle, nothing more that he could tell—it was what the old cowboy movies called a flesh wound, or at least he hoped it was.

Bastard hurt, though.

He knelt back on his heels and thought about things awhile, not wanting to move until he knew what he was moving to.

There was no point checking Manetti or Harrison. He was close enough to see them and there was plenty of moonlight, and you got so you could recognize a dead man as easily as a dog lying dead in the highway, a kind of displaced emptiness hanging over them like a broken TV in a junkyard.

Their deaths disgusted him like Caggiano's had disgusted him. All brave good boys gone long before their time.

Miles Harrison was their newspaper boy.

Remember, Mary?

There wasn't time to mourn them. Any of them.

The .38 was the first thing.

It had gone flying when the kid hit him but it couldn't have gone far.

He took off his jacket, shook the broken glass out of it and brushed it off his shirt, then tied its arms over the wound in his side, knotted it and knelt in the brush, feeling with his hands to the right and left, moving slightly deeper, feeling again over the cool hard-packed earth and lightly around the thorny, woody stems of brush, deeper by a foot and then two feet and then three, being patient, cursing the sharp pangs in his chest and side but still patient, until finally his hand brushed the smooth barrel of the gun. He pushed his way slowly back through the brush and sat down.

When his breathing was even again he stood up and holstered the gun and walked over to Harrison and Manetti. There was a sticky pool of dried blood a few feet away from Manetti that didn't correspond to either his position or Harrison's.

So you got one, Vic, he thought. *I almost would have bet you'd have managed that.*

And I'll bet they took whoever you got home with them too.

He could see that they'd moved quickly, while the body was still doing plenty of bleeding. It left a nice clean trail to follow. His vision wasn't what it used to be but he'd done enough hunting in his day to handle this one.

Got a head wound or neck wound here, he thought, judging from the amount of blood. Whoever was carrying it was swinging the body back and forth, probably hauled up on his shoulder, the body swaying with his gait. Blood not only spotted the path but also sprayed leaves in the brush beside him and farther on, the trunks of trees.

He looked at his watch. An hour and a quarter or more he'd been lying there.

Shit.

He walked back to the rim of the hill. He could see the house lights below. There were squad cars down there now, seven or eight sets of headlights and red-and-blue flashers. But nobody coming his way that he could see. It was tough to know for sure because the tops of trees obscured the field. They could be out there, maybe not far away. They might not.

He considered his options.

From here to the cliffs was basically flatland, and

that he could handle. Going down to meet them at the house or the field was going to be harder. A whole lot harder.

Not the getting down—that he could handle, too—but the getting back up again. It had been bad enough when he wasn't leaking blood all over the place.

He could describe to the troopers with a good deal of accuracy where this had happened. But it was still going to take them time to find it.

Time for him to haul himself down over the hills. Time for him to tell the story. Time to point the way.

Time these people likely didn't have.

To hell with it, he thought.

They had an hour and fifteen minutes' lead on him. They might not be out of earshot yet, but it would still be safe to fire. There wouldn't be any sense of immediate danger to them, nothing that would cause them to panic and start in killing people. They'd know that whoever it was was way back. Could be a hunter for all they knew.

He pointed the .38 into the air and fired, waited until the echo died away and fired again, waited and fired a third time.

The breeze was down considerably and the air was still. If there were any kind of cops worth their pay down there they should be able to take a rough estimate of his position.

Anyhow, it was the best he could do.

With all the activity the wound in his side was doing too much bleeding. It might just kill him after all. With a knife wound deep as that you never knew. He tied the jacket tighter.

He dug into his pocket and filled the empty chambers of the gun.

No more shooting till the shooting starts, he thought, and began to follow.

12:12 A.M.

The Woman entered the cave and let the man drop before the fire. By then the man was willing to drop.

She took it in—the woman clutching her robe by the Cow in the back of the cave. The second woman lying on the floor, bruised, her face bloody, dress torn. Looking up terrified at the twin boys standing over her. The boys grinning red, blue and silver.

And no infant except for Second Stolen's, mewling by the wall.

And no Eartheater. And no Rabbit.

Who should have been here long before her.

First Stolen approached the Woman cautiously, knowing she was angry. She could see that he had been hurt somehow and was mending. She did not care how or why.

All she felt was anger.

He had found the woman, but not the child. She could not understand why.

She sensed the spirit of the other child, hungry for release.

"Rabbit?"

He shook his head, confused. Was Rabbit not with her?

She pushed past him to Second Stolen. The girl was squatting by the fire. The Woman could smell what was boiling in the pot. The lungs, the kidneys, the liver.

"Find Rabbit," she said to the girl. "Eartheater is dead. Find Rabbit."

Second Stolen glanced down into the pot. That Eartheater was her daughter and was dead held no interest for her. She was hungry for the rest of her kill. The Woman knew this.

"*Now,*" she said.

She watched Second Stolen rise and step past the man at the entrance.

The man did not respond or even raise his head.

"Wait," she said.

She walked over to her and handed her the gun that had killed Eartheater in the woods and saw her face change, saw the sullen look disappear as this privilege became clear to her. The Woman knew that First Stolen watched and would be angry.

It didn't matter.

First Stolen would be angry because she had brought the man here, too—the wolf—who looked up from his exhaustion now with eyes that only incompletely masked his hate and fear of her.

"Steven!"

The voice was a hoarse whisper, filled with pain.

She saw his eyes shift to the woman on the floor.
And in them, recognition.

Nothing since he'd run from the police seemed exactly real to Steven. The shadowy woman behind him
in the stream, the sudden detonation of pain and
slack, broken uselessness of his ankle—and then her
return, being helped almost considerately to this
place by some scarred foul-smelling Amazon with a
knife and a pair of pistols in her belt. . . .

This place.

This roost for chickens. This pigsty. Some goddamn armed medieval fortress. Hole in the wall.

An outhouse.

Hell, it was all of them.

And it didn't belong in the real world, he had
dropped through some sick black filthy hole in space
where human arms and legs dangled from the ceiling
and the smell of something sweet and meaty in the
pot mingled with the stink of shit and urine, where
roaches the size of your fist scuttled across the floor
across a naked baby sleeping on a filthy blanket and
up the blackened legs of something with a penis
chained to the back wall.

And in the midst of all this was your wife, beat to hell
and being guarded by a pack of kids. The ultimate
playground fantasy.

Let's get teacher.

"Steven!"

He could have killed her.

241

Jesus! The woman was a stupid bitch! You could bet the farm there was nothing to gain by acknowledging she knew him—and who knew what you stood to lose. Especially since it was pretty damn clear she was not exactly on their good side at the moment.

"Shut the fuck up, Claire," he said.

Temporarily at least that did the trick.

But the woman wasn't stupid—the woman had got the message, all right. She was looking at him, amused and curious.

But she wasn't asking. Not right away at least.

And now he saw Claire's old buddy, Amy, hugging her knees in the back of the cave, almost unrecognizable at first with all that blood smeared over her face, and he wondered where her husband David was.

Where Luke was.

Luke was a pain in the ass but he wasn't a bad kid, really.

He hoped he'd gotten away, actually.

And as for David . . . well, he hoped that David was out there too. For other reasons.

He wasn't being generous. They'd both had it in for him for a long time, David and Amy. The bastards. Loaning Claire money for a lawyer, to pay her bills, whatever. He couldn't feel too bad for either of them if they dropped dead on the spot but the fact was that they were still *like* him, they were civilized people who at least were not living in a shit pile with bones and dead bodies lying around in a goddamn fucking *cave*. You could reason with them, you could get *around* them.

But *these* people . . .

Maybe David would get to the police.

Jail didn't seem so bad right now. Not even on Murder One.

At least there were people inside.

But *these* fuckers . . .

These fuckers scared him.

Like this girl, here.

She was what? maybe ten or eleven years old and she was peeling off the skin she was wearing, unwrapping it and dropping it as she walked back to the guy in the rear of the cave, then grabbing a knife and poking him, cutting him until the guy started to shriek, high-pitched like the girl herself might shriek if she were the one getting jabbed with the thing, little rivulets of blood flowing—and this kid is fucking *laughing*. Amusing herself! And nobody else is paying any attention to them at all except for the baby, who is all of a sudden wailing.

And Marion said *he* was sick sometimes.

At least when he did what he did he had some reason for it. Some damn thing to be gained.

Otherwise it was just craziness, wasn't it?

It wasn't human.

So like it or not what he had here were a couple of allies in Claire and Amy. People he knew. People whose strengths and weaknesses he could depend upon. Even if they were beat all to hell they might still serve as allies in a way. They could help him get by.

There was only one thing to do with your allies.

You used them.

* * *

Amy heard the baby cry and looked up angrily, instinctively at the man in chains and the girl who tormented him. Their noise had disturbed the baby, released its voice—sounds of hunger and distress that caused her breasts to ache again and her heart to pound, wishing for Melissa. She saw that the girl had somehow anticipated her, was already watching her, something dreamy and removed in her eyes yet calculating too, as though she were staring down the short dead-end road of her imagination and trying hard to see farther.

The girl smiled and tossed away the knife and watched his body fall back exhausted against the wall of the cave.

She turned to Amy. She stared for a moment and then turned away.

She walked over to the baby.

And she knew *before she actually knew* what the girl was going to do—her entire body said *no* to this—she knew because the baby was crying loudly and the baby's mother was gone, sent away out of the cave, and she, Amy, was there instead with breasts filled with milk aching to betray her and to betray Melissa.

She shook her head *no* and felt a deep anxious churning inside her as the girl dropped the screaming baby into her arms, into her lap, and the baby clutched her breast through the open robe and took it in a mouth smeared with drool, crusted with dirt, and bit and sucked, pulled deep, its eyes a cold fixed squint that reminded her of the eyes of snakes, its tiny jaws fierce, pulling, grinding, sucking not just milk but the strength and life from her and racking her body with sobs.

She held the baby and cried and felt its pull like the tide, the surge of life. Violent, strange.

Greedy.

Rabbit crouched, poised in the blackberry brambles, the pupils of his eyes widely dilated, watching the rabbit forage for food.

It was not the berries the rabbit was interested in but the tender leaves and shoots, gray in the moonlight. Unaware and upwind, it was moving closer to him all the time. In a moment it would be within striking distance. He would flick his finger, a tiny movement. The rabbit would hear. And then it would only be a matter of which way the rabbit would jump. The rabbit would give away its intent, tilt its narrow head to the right or to the left in that split second before its hind legs gripped and pushed, and by then Rabbit's arms would be there, avoiding the powerful hind legs, ready to grip the ears and upper body and twist its neck.

He had hunted these brambles many times at night and most often he was successful. They formed a thicket on top the cliff high above and to the right of the cave—well away from the easier, more traveled path the others took. But the others were not the hunter Rabbit was. They had never troubled to find this place.

He had brought Eartheater and the Girl here once, but neither could be content just to sit and watch and wait. They had made fun of him, of his grin, of his patient crouch. They made so much noise that no game would dare appear, not even a stupid squirrel. He had waited all night long after they left and returned with nothing.

He wouldn't make the mistake of asking them again.

He remembered that he could not ask Eartheater again, not even if he wanted to. Her body lay a few yards behind him hidden in the bushes beside the trail. He had been here for a while watching the rabbit, though he had only intended to stop for a moment just to see what was here, and he had not wanted the stink of death to frighten any game nearby so he had left it there, covered by sticks and tall grass to cut the scent. He knew it was much later now but he had little sense of time and the rabbit was near.

He felt immensely happy here amid the berries and their cane-like, thorny stems, smelling the woods smell and the rabbit's hide, his feet dug into the earth and his weight distributed between hands and feet to give him balance and the fastest possible lunge. He knew exactly how far his spring would take him, in which direction the brambles would get in his way, and in which direction they would impede the leap of the rabbit. He knew the firmness of the ground, where it was soft and where it was stony, and waited for the rabbit to arrive at exactly the spot that was most to his advantage. These variables were not considered, they were calculated plus or minus in the flesh—in the soles of his feet and the palms of his hands, in his eye and ear. They ran in his blood.

And the moment was almost on him when the rabbit started, nose twitching as it sniffed the air, and the boy heard behind him faraway heavy footfalls along the path, and heard a man panting. He knew from the sounds that it was not one of his kind. He remembered Eartheater's body in the brush and heard the man stop for a long moment and knew that he had found her. Knew that he had delayed here far too long.

He saw the legs of the man pass by as he searched the path near the cliff and as the rabbit ran off deep into the brambles.

He heard him stop at the very edge of the cliff and then return to retrace his steps. He smelled the man and recalled the smell, knew it for the smell of death because he had killed the man only a while ago with his knife.

And yet he walked.

He huddled shaking in the thicket, a Rabbit in truth now for the very first time, shuddering, frozen in fear, while the ghost went slowly down the mountain.

Through waves of throbbing pain Claire watched the tall scarred woman kneel down to Steven and search his eyes, studying him, her head tilted like an animal's, inquisitive.

Like a cat's.

She was aware of the twins and the boy with the clouded eye looking to the man for instructions, anxious for permission, probably, to go on kicking her and beating her again. She was aware of their mouths and what was in them. Very aware. But the man was watching Steven too, ignoring them.

247

She was aware of Amy crying.

She saw a roach crawl to the top of one of the rocks banking the fire and fall in, overcome by heat, crackling.

But mostly she was aware of the woman.

She could feel something in this woman that was missing in the others. She sensed it powerfully. A thoroughly dangerous oneness, a wholeness with what she was, like a tiger or panther feeding—a total concentration of energy that was completely *of the animal*, intent and undistractible.

The woman leaned close.

She saw that Steven could not even meet her eyes.

"The baby," she said.

There was ferocity in the question. There was blood. Claire felt it like a cold blast of wind.

Steven looked puzzled.

"Hers," said the woman quietly. She pointed to the back of the cave.

And now he understood.

"I don't know," he said.

And she could see that not knowing scared him.

She watched him look away from the woman, considering, and then after a while look back at her. Not once did the woman's eyes blink or waver, though Steven's roamed the walls, the fire, the ceiling, lingered for a moment on the twin boys and the one with the clouded eye, and even—however briefly—on Claire. But now when they returned to the woman Claire knew he had arrived at something, at some decision, he could meet the woman's gaze now, if only for a moment.

She had seen that look before.

And she didn't know which of them—Steven or the woman—was more to be feared.

He glanced at the boys again. At their smiling open mouths.

"I don't know," he said. "But I think you can find out."

He looked at Claire.

"She doesn't like," he said, "to be bitten."

12:25 A.M.

Claire stared at him in shock.

The man had been her husband.

They had made love night after night and it had been good, once, she had believed it was good.

They had made a baby together, had considered having another.

They had skied in Vermont and weekended at the shore.

She doesn't like to be bitten.

Claire heard the words. It was still nearly impossible to believe he'd said them—dead calm and dead serious, as though it were not her life and maybe Luke's he was talking about, as though he were simply making a suggestion to a client who had a certain problem and this was the solution which, after due consideration of the variables, he'd come up with.

He nodded toward the boys. "You have all you need," he said, "right here."

So this is who you are, thought Claire.

Beneath the panic, she hated him.

You know too much, damn you. About me, about the situation. And you have no soul. You will betray anything.

He knew that Luke was out there somewhere, the only one they hadn't found yet.

He knew that Claire would never have abandoned Amy's baby.

So the baby was with Luke. And probably, Claire knew where.

He was suggesting that they find Melissa through Luke, and Luke through her. He was suggesting pain. That pain would result in betrayal.

Of his son.

She doesn't like to be bitten.

Simple fact.

Almost ludicrous.

And true enough about Claire in its mundane, everyday way to be almost elemental, almost monstrous.

She didn't like to be tickled either god knows or touched on the soles of her feet or the taste of raw onions or rainy winter days or the smell of whiskey or of gasoline at the pump. These were just facts about her. Items in the catalog of her personality. Amy knew them. David knew them. Luke knew them.

Yet this one went deeper, drew on a confidence shared with him and few others that in some ways defined the physical limits of her power over fear, and her moral courage in the face of it.

It was not onions or whiskey. It was horror. It went to the heart of her knowledge of herself. And he had given it over as casually as if he'd been asked about the color of her hair.

Who is worse? she thought. *Which one? The man who reveals the secret or the woman who would use it against her?* Because she had no doubt that the woman would use it. The woman was staring at the boys—and the boys had reminded Steven in the first place.

They had kicked her but their feet were bare thank god because there was pain but the damage was not too bad, not compared to the man's pain where she had kicked him, and he had rolled off the floor and groaned, telling them to stop.

They obeyed, walking away from her to the side of the cave, the boy with the clouded eye rummaging through a pile and handing to the others two sets of jagged teeth cut roughly from the sides of soda cans and keeping one for himself, placing it in his mouth so that the rounded rim of the can slid up between his lips and upper gums and the sharp teeth pointed down.

They had stood over her, mouths open, the tang of aluminum making them drool down over their chins. Waiting. For the man to allow them.

The woman stood in front of her and reached for her, hauled her to her feet as easily as though she were an empty sack, her rough hands abrasive beneath her arms, stood her up and pushed her against the wall.

"Say," she said.

The eyes bored into her, the breath raw as old meat, the smooth scar livid against her gray pallor.

The man stood behind her in the shadows. Smiling.

His teeth too. Rotted brown and black and filed to sharp points.

The children moved closer.

She felt the room begin to spin, her pores opening and the smell of her own sweat coming off her all at once and her stomach turned, it was as though she had drunk too much, she was going to be sick all over the woman and then the woman would kill her and maybe that was for the best, she wouldn't have to tell, she wouldn't have to say.

"Say," the woman repeated.

She saw teeth and fire and the bright scar, and for a moment couldn't have told her if she'd wanted to. The room slid into white light and the wet surface of a dimly lit suburban Boston street when she was ten years old. It was dusk and she was visiting her cousin Barbara and they and her cousin's friends were playing hide-and-seek and she was it and she had found the others but she couldn't find Barbara so she crawled under the cyclone fence to the neighbors' yard where the bushes against the fence made it shadowy and scary, a good place for her cousin to hide, being careful not to dirty her short dress, but Barbara wasn't there either so she turned to go under the fence again because she didn't like being there in the shadows, when a dog appeared from around the side of the house, a big dog, old and black, and she could tell by looking at him standing there that he was going to bite. There was something in his eyes.

She had heard that an animal would attack if you moved so she didn't, she stood still, hoping it would just go away but the animal held her with its stare—there was something wrong with its eyes, a thin ugly film like the whites of eggs—and by the time the dog moved, trotting over to her, never letting go of her with its eyes, crazy looking, not like the eyes of any dog she'd ever seen, she was shaking and she had to go pee and the dog just stopped in front of her. Opened its mouth. And took the flesh of the front of her naked thigh into its warm wet jaws. Slowly, deliberately.

And bit down.

She half screamed and half cried and she couldn't help it, her leg moved back a little. The dog bit deeper, and there was blood rolling down her leg, a single warm stream.

The dog looked up into her eyes. Growled.

And bit harder.

She knew she was looking into the face of evil then, into the face and eyes of madness, of something that enjoyed her pain more than anything else its life could offer, and she wet herself and whimpered and suddenly a man's voice thundered off the porch and the dog let go and ran, and she ran, screaming—and when she got to the house and told her mother, her mother wanted her to go back to confront the man with what the dog had done but she was still too scared and she couldn't, her mother had to go get the man to show him.

The man was old. He was stooped and small. Much too small to have such a loud mean voice that would scare the dog that way. But then they heard the man later, shouting, something smashing against the walls, and the dog yelping wildly.

"Say," said the woman.

"I don't know," she said. "I swear I don't."

The woman looked at Steven. He shook his head.

The woman's hands tightened on her arms, the jagged nails digging in.

"All right. The house. I told Luke to go back to the

255

house if anything . . . if anything happened to me. To take Melissa with him and go back to the house right away."

Steven smiled. *He knows me too well,* she thought, goddamn him. He could always tell.

"The truth, Claire," he said. "Go on. Tell her."

I can't do this, she thought.

There was only one place where she thought Luke might be and that was the treehouse. It was just as possible he wasn't there—he could be *anywhere,* even safe by now—but if there was one place more likely than any other it was the treehouse. He'd found it. He'd felt secure enough there to show her so they could hide.

I can't do this, she thought. *I can't risk it. I can't let them know.*

The woman saw her refusal, read her clearly, put the palm of her hand against her breastbone and slammed her against the wall. The woman's hands went to her shoulders, bunching the fabric of the wide neck of her dress in her hands, and tore it off her shoulders. She reached down for Claire's wrists and dragged her in front of the fire and threw her down again, the skin of her hands and knees scraping off on the hard stone floor, her naked breasts suddenly cold against its clammy touch.

The woman stepped over her, put her foot in the small of her back and tore away the cotton briefs.

Hands grasped her arms and legs and rolled her over.

Hands held her, spread her arms and legs wide and she fought them but she was weak, faces with Halloween fangs leaned over her and she looked into those faces at those fangs and was suddenly as weak as the dog had made her so very long ago, she cried and screamed and no one stopped her but no one comforted her either as her mother had comforted her and the faces leaned down, slowly, mouths opening, leaning closer, and she felt the first flesh tearing in the hot mouth of the boy with the clouded eye holding her ankle, felt them sear into her calf and saw that the girl was holding her other ankle and that she too had teeth now, and then felt the slow incisions on each side of her in the tender webbing of flesh that joined shoulder to breast above each armpit before the girl's teeth sank into her thigh above her knee, the flaming pain from all four points scorching up and through her.

She felt their tongues lap and the cool spill of saliva and blood, and heard them swallow.

She screamed and thrashed her head as the jaws worked side to side.

She screamed for Steven. She screamed for god. She did not know what she screamed.

And then there was only the man—the man and her terrible sudden impossible knowledge of what he meant to do as she looked down over her body and felt his hands grip her thighs and pull himself toward her through her open legs, using her own bruised flesh as purchase, crawling along on his belly as slowly as a snake gliding toward her, his mouth open wide, saliva dripping from his teeth and head lowering, the humid heat of his breath over her as he sought her inches away.

I'm sorry, Luke, she thought. *I'm not going to tell them*

257

but I'm not going to be here for you either, anymore. I'm sorry, I'm very sorry.

She closed her eyes as the mouth descended.

They met at the base of the cliff—and Peters was just coming off the rock face into the sand thinking *the legs are the first to go* when the girl stepped out from behind the brush, the police-issue .38 pointed at him, and he took it in.

He wobbled and stumbled but he took it in.

The girl had no experience with a gun; she held it in front of her straight-arm like a kid in the general direction of his body, aiming at mass, not target. She was certain to jerk the trigger and keep on jerking it, and that was what she did.

So that the stumble worked for him—the stumble was a goddamn blessing. He hit his knees and righted himself and took the position as the first bullet kicked sand and seashells to the left of him and fired as the second bullet whizzed past his head. The third went straight to the stars because his own shot had taken her in the chest by then, and the girl went down not four feet away from him and got right up again like some cardboard duck in a shooting gallery but she'd lost control of the trigger, her finger was trying to find it when he fired point-blank into her chest again and put her down.

The gun sailed away into the sand. Peters got to his feet and walked over.

He looked down at her and shook his head.

Because it was the same as eleven years ago in a way. Faced with the kind of slaughter the like of which he'd never seen or ever dreamed of seeing, it still wasn't so much the killing that got to him—except for the boy, because the boy was his fault, his problem—as it was knowing who and what these people were. Like some other species entirely, one that had evolved along parallel lines maybe, but whose ancestors in the Pleistocene or whenever the hell they'd done their evolving were not *his* ancestors or those of anybody he'd ever heard of, had taken a turn that was impossible for him to understand. He knew it wasn't true, that there were guys like Manson and Bundy out there too. But he had never met them either, and if he lived to be a hundred he would never understand.

He would never understand.

He watched her lying there, the last of her life draining out into the sand, her pale hands quivering, moving up over her body until her fingers found the entrance wounds beneath the dirty, bloody shirt.

And then weakly, *probing*.

And the goddamn girl was smiling.

Second Stolen lay bathed in the warm wet pleasure that was pain.

She remembered, long ago, a man who was dressed very much like this man who stood over her now, who was heavy like this man. And more dimly, she remembered the woman who was his mate. A thin worn face in contrast to the man's heavy face, with eyes that were mild and perhaps a little distracted, a little hurt and empty, but were not at all like the man's pig eyes, who did not have the man's heavy calloused hands, the hands that probed and beat her.

She smiled, remembering how she had escaped the man, how the Woman had come into her room in the night and taken her.

The Woman was young then. Second Stolen was just a child.

She had not understood. She had cried and cried and the Woman had left her in the dark.

Sensation entered her more deeply than it did the others.

Her fingers could feel the heat inside her, the warm wet life, the smooth pulsing. The familiar pain that told her who she was.

Slowly, the memory faded.

The ghost had led him here for this.

To watch them below, to hear and smell the gunfire and watch Second Stolen fall.

To demonstrate its power by making him follow. And see.

He had imagined the idea was his own.

Rabbit hid in the shadows behind a ledge of rock and saw the man's ghost stand over her, reach down and touch the base of her throat and then move on lumbering like a bear across the sand in the direction of the cave and thought, *He has gone to hunt them all.*

All of them.

It did not occur to him as strange that a ghost should use a gun or breathe so heavily.

He only felt panic at the *lure* of the ghost—strong enough to bring him here, to bring Second Stolen from out of the safety of the cave so it could kill her, as quickly as a snake striking a rabbit.

He turned and scrambled up the rock face.

He did not use the path the ghost had walked but ran instead through the woods, off the trail that bore its scent—and when he heard the voices of the men and realized that they were many, all coming toward him, all from the same direction yet spread wide across the hills, when he smelled them and the oil of their weapons, he could only hide again downwind in the thicket and hope that they would pass as the ghost had passed and leave him alone and free.

There was another, better place to hide if he could reach it. He and Eartheater and the Boy had used it often. Not far.

He could wait high above them all in safety.

He could watch from high above throughout the night and even the next day.

Not far.

"Here! Over here!"

Peters' gun was ready—but this just wasn't one of them.

This was a boy, just an ordinary boy, *like the one he had shot eleven years ago and no way was he going to make that mistake again*—a boy hunched in the tall grass at the base of the cliff, waving at him.

The boy was dirty and bloody, his face and hands scratched up bad, wearing wet pajamas and frantically waving, hissing at Peters in a bad excuse for a whisper and *that close* to crying.

The boy looked scared to death.

But he was alive.

Peters promised himself he was going to get to stay that way.

"Where are they?" he said.

The boy pointed. A slice of pure black in the rock above. A fissure.

A cave.

"Up there," the boy said.

It was going to be a hell of a climb. The wound in his side was leaking him away. Worse than he'd thought.

"Who's with them?"

"My . . . my mom. And Amy, maybe. I think Amy."

"Who's Amy?"

"My mom's friend. Mrs. Halbard."

"You saw them?"

"I saw my mom. And I think . . . maybe . . ."

"Who, son?"

The boy looked confused.

". . . I think I saw my *father*," he said. "There was somebody else. It was later. There was a man with a woman, and he was leaning on her and they were going up and it looked like . . . but my father's in his apartment in New York I think so it couldn't . . . I don't . . ."

And he realized the kid had followed them. Then stayed there to keep an eye on the place. That meant he was looking at a pretty determined, pretty resourceful, pretty resilient kid. He was shaking like a leaf. It wasn't his wet clothes. Peters didn't blame him.

The boy's confusion brought tears finally and Peters was damn near glad to see them. Tears were normal. Tears were right.

He put his hand on the boy's shoulder and squatted down.

It hurt like hell but he did it anyway.

"That's real good work, son," he said. "Now listen. I'm going up there and I want you to stay right here out of sight and watch for me. You hide out right in this grass, okay? And if anybody comes along that doesn't look right to you, you stay where you are. You hide. You don't need to worry about me for a second. You don't need to warn me, you don't need to do anything but hide. I'll be fine. And if anybody comes along who looks like a policeman, you show 'em where I've got to. There are gonna be policemen coming and we're going to get everybody out of here in fine shape. Okay?"

The boy wiped his nose and nodded.

"Now we just met but I get the feeling you're a pretty brave guy," he said. "You hang in there and watch for those uniforms and I'll see you soon, okay? Go on, get down now."

The boy nodded again and his eyes were dry.

It was good, Peters thought, to give the kid a purpose.

Hell, up until last night he'd probably needed one himself.

There were entirely too many strangers around these days.

See you, Mary, he thought. He started up the rock face.

He was only a quarter of the way up when he heard the woman's screams.

12:35 A.M.

Amy heard Claire's screams, and they pitched her out of her deep tidal fog into the unsteady light of the cave.

She saw herself holding the thing at her breast, cradling it in her arms while it squeezed and sucked. Her nipple an angry red.

She wiped the thick congealed blood from her eyes and saw Claire on the floor writhing, struggling, the children leaning over her like the black shapes of bats, their elbows askew.

She heard lapping, feeding.

She saw Steven watching passively, and the woman standing over them.

And saw the man crawl forward between Claire's legs like some huge lumbering iguana, then raise his head and strike as suddenly Claire lurched to the side so that his teeth sunk into her inner thigh and the man began to shake, working free the flesh between his teeth while she screamed and pitched with all her strength, tearing free of the boy at her right arm, his metal teeth lodged in her shoulder and the blood pouring down while the man threw back his head and opened his mouth and swallowed—*bolted her*—and suddenly she was Claire and Claire was Amy, and the thing at her breast was all of them.

She pulled herself up against the back wall of the cave and tore its mouth away, felt filaments of spittle cold against her breast, and thrust the screeching thing high above her head.

"Stop! Stop it!" she screamed. She felt the caked blood crack along her face.

"What are you, fucking *crazy?*"

Steven was by the fire, trying to stand, his leg going out from under him. "Amy, put it the hell *down* for chrissakes! You do that they'll kill us!"

But they *had* stopped. They were off her.

Looking at Amy.

Even the man had stopped and turned.

"Kill us?" There was the urge to laugh. The urge to hysteria. "They'll kill us anyway, Steven. Look at her. *Look* goddammit! Look at what they've done to your wife you stinking piece of *shit!*"

"I don't have a wife." He shrugged, looked at Claire. "You mean this? Fuck it," he said.

The woman stepped forward.

"Don't!"

She raised the baby higher. It wriggled in her grasp. It wanted to get free. She felt a split second of guilt for using it this way, and the woman must have seen it in her eyes—something weakening for a moment, hesitant—because she took another step and the others were slowly rising too and there was nowhere to go, no cards to play but the baby.

Don't make me, she thought.

You don't know me—and you don't know me and Claire.

"Stay where you are," she said.

She was aware of Steven half crawling, half stumbling to the entrance to the cave and Claire rolling over on her side, weeping, as the others halted and then began to move again.

And it was slow, the tempo of a dream, a nightmare glide that brought them together as a pack, the children covered with Claire's blood, the man's chin glistening. She heard the *snick* of a knife pulled out of its sheath and saw it appear in the girl's hand, saw a razor in the hand of one of the twins. She heard the rattle of chains and realized that she had edged nearer the naked man, was aware of him watching with interest and straining against his chains, grunting, caught fascinated in the wake of the wholly unfamiliar.

"Don't," she said.

The woman stopped, reached for the gun in her belt and Amy knew two things simultaneously—that it was exactly the gun she needed and that this was the single chance she'd ever get to try.

Forgive me, she thought.

And the baby seemed to know because it screamed as her hands tightened and her arms moved back. She threw it hard and blindly somewhere beyond the woman, somewhere into the pack and saw its limbs splay out, its body tumble as the woman whirled and the twins and the boy with the clouded eye reached for it and someone—the boy—caught it by one naked outstretched arm and pulled it roughly toward him.

The woman whirled again, snarling, but by then Amy was on her, diving clumsily into her midsection because that was where the gun was, staggering her only slightly but groping, searching for the gun, tugging it out of her belt as the woman chopped her down with a fist, then rolling dazzled by the blow toward the fire and bringing the gun up and pointing it at where she was. Except the woman wasn't there anymore. She rolled and the woman was gone. The woman was on the far side of the cave picking up an ax, running toward her again and so was the man and the children and she didn't know where to shoot, they were all coming at her at once so she just pulled and pulled the trigger.

The echoes pounded through the cave and she saw the man reach out for her and sway as the bullets impacted his chest like thrown mud, flesh and blood splattering the girl beside him. One of the twins had fallen, clutching his knee. The man lurched forward and she fired again and suddenly the gun was empty, the hammer falling on empty chambers as the woman raised her arms and the man gripped the sleeve of her robe and then its collar with his dripping bloody hands and bent her back, turning her, presenting her body to the woman and the ax.

There was poetry in here somewhere.

Peters recognized him instantly. Muddy suit and all.

The man looked pretty shocked, though, seeing Peters.

OFFSPRING

He was wasting neither words nor bullets by then.

He just let the man have it with the butt end of the .38 and watched him crumble.

He was walking a deer-path ledge fifteen feet from the crease in the rock that the boy had said was the entrance to the cave. It was right in front of him.

I'm going in again, Mary, he thought. *Just like eleven years ago. Just like the night they got Caggiano, and I got the boy.*

This is what kept us up all those nights.

This is what you had to suffer through just in order to stay with me.

You wish me luck, Mary. You give me a hand here.

Maybe this time, I'll get it right.

He was a few steps back when somebody inside opened fire and he didn't wait for it to finish. He just stepped on in.

The pain was brittle.

Each blast of gunfire seemed to fracture a bone in Claire.

She had been trying to rise when the man walked in. The pain almost sat her down again.

But she watched him pick his shots.

He seemed to size up everything in an instant, stepping around her, near her, crouching, the waves of tension pouring off him flooding her with a wild new joy of her own, that finally the nightmare was for *them*, not for Claire and Amy—for *them!*—and when he fired and she saw the man's eye disappear, saw Amy drop from his grasp, saw the wide black hole where the eye was and saw his head jerk back and the gleaming wet wall

269

behind him, she watched him fall and had all she could do to keep her hands off this grim old man with the gun, all she could do to not embrace him.

Amy was on her hands and knees. He fired again. The woman went down spinning beside her, the ax clattering against the wall.

He fired again as the boy with the clouded eye leaped across the fire. The children were everywhere now, scattered, moving fast. Even the twin with the shattered knee was dragging himself across the floor, slicing the air with his razor. And the man would have hit the boy, she thought, had not the boy's foot caught the handle of the pot boiling on the fire so that he twisted in midair, fell beneath the bullet's path, his left leg kicking up the flames and showering them with sparks.

The pot spilled across the floor, steaming. Gray broth scalded the soles of her feet.

She pulled herself up and away, standing, shaking. As David's lungs and kidneys disgorged themselves from the pot in front of her and the man fired once again.

The leg of the boy's pants was going up in flames but he didn't notice, he didn't care, the knife was raised and he lunged as the man fired point-blank into his face. She turned so as not to see and glimpsed Amy on her feet, staggering toward her—and between them the crippled twin with the razor, the one whose knee Amy's bullet had smashed. Dragging the leg, trying to reach them.

The man shot again and she turned in time to see the second twin fall in a heap against the wall of the cave, but saw too that the man had not escaped him, saw the knife protruding from his shoulder as the girl lurched forward and stabbed him in the chest, twisting the knife one long agonizing moment and sinking it deeper until he managed to lift the gun and fire directly into her ear.

He fell to his knees, clutching the girl's long blade, too weak to pull it away. His face was covered with her blood.

He looked over at Claire and she saw the warning in his eyes a split second before he toppled forward.

She whirled and felt something slash her arm— hot, almost painless—and saw the crippled twin raise his arm to strike a second time and Amy suddenly behind him, reaching into his dirty matted hair, her full weight pushing him forward facedown into the dense-packed embers beside her.

The boy struggled, sparks flying, his hair bursting into flame, and Claire *felt* Amy's hands burning too, felt it as though her own were burning but she wouldn't let go, she held him—it felt like they *both* were holding him—until the boy's screaming struggles stopped and his face lay sizzling in the fire like charring meat.

Claire lifted her up.

But for the sounds from the fire and the rattle of chains the cave was silent.

From somewhere in the shadows she heard the baby cry.

Tears and the black residue of greasy smoke streaked Amy's face. Her hands were black where they were not burned white. She held them helplessly out in front of her.

"It's all right," Claire said. "It's over."

She looked at the man who had saved them, his hands still gripping the handle of the knife. His eyes were motionless, half-open. She couldn't tell if he was breathing or not.

She felt a pang of loss, of something almost like love for the man. The man was a total stranger. Among them for a matter of moments. She felt it anyway. That somehow his being here wasn't by accident, that some deeply human impulse had drawn him here to help them. And maybe it wasn't too late. Maybe they could still return the favor.

"We've got to get out of here," she said. "We've got to find someone."

There was a pile of blankets behind her. She took one for herself and one for Amy. The blankets were crusted hard and smelled of urine but both of them were trembling uncontrollably and she knew enough to cover them to guard against shock.

The wound in her thigh was a constant agony and she was walking in her own streaming blood. For a while she had almost forgotten the wound.

She wrapped the blankets around them.

"Come on," she said.

In the fire the boy's face popped and sizzled.

They walked out into the warm moonlit night.

She saw Steven lying on the path a few feet from the entrance to the cave.

She felt nothing at all on seeing him there, not even any curiosity as to whether he was dead or alive. She felt more for the man lying stabbed and bleeding inside.

Steven belonged with the dead now. In more ways than one.

Not Amy, though, she thought, and hugged her tighter. *And not me. And not that man inside.*

And when she heard Luke's voice down the mountain—his bad stage whisper, and the men's deeper voices hushing him—she felt something soar out of her like a nesting gull, and knew that what she lacked time would somehow endow again, and it was almost possible to smile.

12:45 A.M.

Do not try to escape the wound, thought the Woman. *Make it welcome.*

The trick had been taught to her far more years ago than she could remember. Once before it had saved her life—and it had always made her impervious to pain.

She took the wound into her—even locating and including the bullet that lay pressed to the back of her seventh rib—surrounded it, encompassed it. Until the invaded flesh was no more or less consequential to her than a fingernail or a follicle of hair.

And finally was able to rise.

She stood, the damp air thick with the smell of gunfire, and calmly surveyed the cave.

The children were dead.

First Stolen, dead.

She would have to begin again.

She kicked the fat man twice in the belly and saw

the last of the breath in him huff out between his lips with the first sharp blow.

She looked down into his face as she had before on the path and knew him again, knew that whoever he was, this man had once inhabited her dreams.

Perhaps he would again, and perhaps the next time she would understand why.

The women, her captives, were gone. She would have to hurry.

The knife was secure in the back of her belt.

She stripped off the bloody shirt and gathered up Second Stolen's child squalling on the floor. At her touch the child went suddenly quiet.

For a moment she noticed its eyes.

Its eyes unnerved her. As though they understood her intent, and approved. Not the eyes of an infant. The eyes had wisdom.

Power.

She wrapped the shirt around it and tied the bottom corners together between its legs, then knotted the arms and slipped them over her head so that the baby hung pressed with its belly to her back behind her shoulders in a makeshift harness, riding high enough so that she could quickly get to the knife. The baby's tiny fingers flexed against her naked back as though seeking purchase in the Woman's flesh, opening and closing against her.

She walked quickly to the back of the cave.

She felt a chill. The body of the other infant, the one who had brought this upon them, lay leaning against the wall in the white plastic garbage bag to the right of the Cow. She could see the side of his face and one shoulder pressed straining into the bag, as though the infant were trying to break free.

Its spirit unreleased.

She had failed in this.

There was no hope for release now but she could still set its vengeance far away from her at least, she could set it into the drifts and deeps of the sea.

She picked up the bag, twisted it, and tied it into her belt.

She reached into the rusted yellow coffee can beside the Cow and found his tethers and his key. She removed the chains and left them dangling. She could find other chains. But the Cow could not be left behind. The Cow was necessary in order to begin again.

She tied the strong gut lines around his wrists, took the lines in one hand and the ax in the other and walked him to the entrance to the cave. Ordinarily she would have walked him backward—his wrists tied behind his back. The Cow had become very adept at walking backward, and it was amusing to watch him stumble. But the trail was narrow and she had no wish to lose him down the mountain or be delayed by his stumbling.

Outside the wind shifted and she smelled salt and tide off the sea. She heard voices. Whispers.

Not yet to the entrance, but close by.

She jerked at the tethers. The Cow grunted and trudged forward.

Outside she listened. She heard footsteps from below. But the path above them was clear.

The warm night air laved the wound at her side. The Cow shuffled to a halt behind her.

The man was sitting dazed in the path a few feet away. He looked up as they approached and removed his hand from the side of his head. The hand came away bloody.

She allowed herself a moment of regret. The man had been useful to her in a small way. Given time, he might have been much more so. She had known the wolf in him would turn ruthless in its own interests, in its own defense.

But the wolf was crippled, unable to escape the voices on the mountain.

It did not seem to know this. It held its hands palms upward to her in supplication and shook its head as it stared into the impassive mask of her face and tried to rise. It whimpered.

Perhaps it sensed her intention. Or perhaps it wished simply not to be left behind.

In either case this was only a man now—the wolf in him had fled.

The wolf was on the wind.

So that it was a kindness to the man to swing the ax, to break swiftly and cleanly through the ear and skull, to send half the skull sailing out into the night down the cliffside to the sand below. She watched the body stir, still sitting, as it slowly began to fall and smelled the sudden metallic smell of blood, tantalizing, intoxicating in the salt air.

The wound in her side wanted feeding.

She realized suddenly that her entire body did. It had been many hours since the kill and feast of the night before, might be many more till it fed again.

She must act quickly.

The steep upward incline would hinder those below for another moment yet.

She caught the shoulders as they fell and brought the body upright, bent over and set her mouth to the broken lip of the skull and drank deep of the blood and fluid that drooled across the rim—rich, thick, salty—her hands holding the neck and chin to steady him, drinking from the still-warm cup of him, intent on this as the child began to wriggle in its makeshift harness and the Cow reached into the back of her belt and silently withdrew the knife.

The Cow stared into the open palm of his hand as though the knife had appeared by magic, not his own volition—as though some miracle had got it there.

In eight years he had seen so many. Knives for skinning and for scraping the skins, for cutting and sectioning meat, and then for feeding. For sharpening sticks or bones like the ones they used to torment him. He had seen knives heated to cauterize wounds or to dig for parasites. Used for killings of animals and men—fast and slow.

Yet he had never held one.

The years in chains had made him weak—all but one organ. And that was rising now as his hand closed over the carved bone handle and the Woman fed.

An image came to him of a man huddled for what must have been weeks in a dark narrow crevice, sealed off from all light and where it was impossible to stand or even kneel, living off the insects that crawled through his feces and the occasional scrap of meat that emerged from the sudden blinding light.

279

The man had a name. Frederick. He could not remember the rest.

But the Woman had put him there, and the Woman had delivered him.

And by then he was the Cow.

All the years in chains had made him weak. But not so weak that he could not take the knife in both hands now and drive it into her back, dimly aware of the child only inches from his hands struggling to crawl free of its harness, pushing forward on the knife with all the miserable weight of his flesh and bone, his erection driving too against the smoothness of her thigh in the most pleasurable sensation of his life.

He squealed, grinning, as she strangled him.

She shook him like a rag doll and soon his tongue protruded but he would not die, the light in his eyes seemed filled with pleasure and it would not go out, and she marveled that the power of the spirit of the dead infant was such that it had caused even this, had first torn the very structure of her world away from her and now even its sense, so that it was hardly even a surprise to her when the guns sounded and her flesh exploded in a dozen places and plunged them both spinning down the mountain.

And the last thing she was aware of was Second Stolen's child torn away from her by the bullets' impact and its eyes, gazing coldly at her and then into the empty night as it fell away. Unafraid.

A huntress.

12:55 A.M.

Rabbit climbed the tree to the platform.

He had waited until the woods were silent, until the men in the woods had passed by and he could hear their feet scuffling on the rocks below. And then he had waited further just to make certain and because he was still afraid.

He was moving through the brush when he heard the guns. So many guns. Then nothing.

He was sure his people were dead.

The important thing now was to stay hidden.

He was Rabbit. Alone now. Learning to be Fox.

He climbed cautiously, his knife between his teeth, aware of unfamiliar scents from above. Not his. Not Eartheater's or the Boy's.

In the stillness they drifted down to him on slow currents of air. It was almost as though they were visible.

He smelled fear.

Faint, distant. A residue.

But pleasing to him.

He smelled *innocence*—the blind security of hatchlings asleep in their nest.

He raised himself up, peered across the platform. His lips curled smiling off the blade.

It was what they had been seeking. Through all this night of amazements and destruction. And he, Rabbit, whom the others laughed at and would not listen to, whose smile had always been a sign for them that he was poorly made somehow, had found it. Asleep in a blanket where he had taken Eartheater and the Boy to play. His place.

He could almost miss them now. There was no one to witness his triumph.

He rolled onto the platform lightly as a breeze and lay there. The infant beside him slept on. Its mouth was open. Its eyes were closed. He leaned in closer. Its breath smelled sweet.

He parted the blanket that covered her legs. The infant was a female.

The Woman had said they must use the infant's blood to quench the spirit thirst of the dead child— and that this was for the good of all of them.

But there was no *all of them* now.

Only Rabbit.

He considered this.

In his mind he could taste its warm sweet blood.

And he could almost, but not quite, imagine the other. But time could make it real.

And he thought that the Woman would approve of his conclusion. That she would not think him quite so stupid after all.

OFFSPRING

The infant was female.

In her, in him, they could begin again.

He had only to wait and hunt and hide. Ten, eleven summers.

The Woman would approve.

He lay beneath a full moon darkened by clouds within the sound of the sea and claimed her.

He reached for the sleeping child, gathered her into his arms and she opened her eyes, knew who she belonged to now, then heard someone running, running hard toward the tree and a voice farther away call for the runner to stop. He listened to the footfalls and thought, *Older, yes, but only another innocent, the boy,* though the voice was a man's voice and much more dangerous, and he crouched and drew the blade.

It wasn't like he felt like a hero or anything, but as soon as Luke got them near the treehouse he started getting excited.

It was as though in all this horrible stuff, with all this going on that made him want to cry and *did* make him cry—his mom and Amy coming hurt so bad down the mountain, the shooting on the mountain, *those people falling so close to where he was standing he could hear them hit like great big sacks of dirt and even the baby falling so that he couldn't look, he couldn't, he just hid behind the policeman,* then asking about his father and nobody answering and the awful sick smell of the blankets his mother wore as she held him, the way she cried, the blood on Amy's face—it was as

283

though in all this awful terrible stuff there was one good thing at least. And that was that Melissa was safe. Melissa was all right.

And he was the one who knew *where* she was because he had put her there. He felt good about that. So that when one of the policemen said okay show us and another said no wait, take care of these people here and we'll call it in and then we'll *all* go, he was glad his mom insisted that they find her right away, right now before something happened to her, that Luke should show them. He was glad even though it was hard to leave her and even though he thought, *What could happen?* These people, they were all dead, weren't they? And Melissa couldn't crawl yet. She couldn't crawl and hurt herself. His mom had said she was still too young for that.

So what could happen?

Animals, he thought.

Animals could get her. That scared him for a while. But he didn't really believe it.

Sure it was possible but it just didn't seem *right* somehow, to have gotten her all this way hidden real well and then have some animal get her. He didn't believe it at all, he *wouldn't* believe it and as he took the group of policemen up the cliff with him the scared feeling went away and he started to feel pretty good. His mom was safe. He was safe. And Melissa was going to be safe, too.

So he was excited when they got to the treehouse—not some hero, but excited.

And he didn't really listen when the officer told him to stop.

"Up here!" he said.

And ran out ahead.

He climbed the steps as fast as he could.

And the policemen were behind him but they were adults and a whole lot slower and had a whole lot less to be excited about, so they hadn't even got to the ladder yet when he was up, his head over the top of the platform and he was grinning, he could hardly wait to see Melissa there . . . when this dark sudden shape of something in front of him hissed and rushed forward, and even before he saw the glint of the knife he lost his footing and cried out and started to fall.

He twisted sideways, trying to hold on to the railing with one arm and flailing with the other and the knife darted past his head. He heard the railing crack as the boy leaned over and tried to stab him but he was still dangling, swinging, trying to grasp hold of something, *anything* solid with his free right hand— and what he found was the wrist with the knife.

He found it by mistake. But he didn't let go because the knife couldn't cut him that way and something told him to *pull* so he did pull and that part of the railing the boy was leaning over cracked again— and suddenly the boy let go of the knife, it tumbled away, and grabbed *his* wrist instead as he broke through the railing and fell, held on to his wrist as he fell the length of him and with his other hand grabbed his leg.

And started to *climb* him.

Agony shot through his arm on the railing. But his feet had found the ladder or else they'd both have fallen.

Luke had never seen a boy so strong and an instant later they were face-to-face. A face so dirty the dirt seemed a part of him.

The boy's breath was hot and it stunk and he was smiling. He saw crazy eyes and twisted brown-black teeth.

The boy had let go of his wrist and had him by the shoulders. He looked up and around and Luke saw what he meant to do, he was going to pull himself up over Luke's shoulders onto the platform and then up the tree, maybe into the next tree then and over and he might even make it in the darkness, it would be hard for the policemen to see.

He heard Melissa crying and thought, *What if he takes Melissa so they can't fire. And then what if he falls?* And in the instant that the boy lifted his hand off Luke's shoulder he got so suddenly mad at him, at all of them and maybe at everybody in the whole damn world who hurt people who never *deserved* to be hurt that he swung his elbow as hard as he could into the middle of the boy's ribs.

As fast as the boy had appeared he was gone.

Faster.

One minute he was there and the next he wasn't. He didn't even scream.

Luke didn't look down.

He didn't need to know if the boy was dead. He could tell by the sound. The sound was the same as the people falling off the rocks.

He didn't like the sound, but he wasn't afraid of it either. Not anymore.

His legs were shaking but he managed the two

more steps up to Melissa okay, and then just sat there trembling and breathing and gradually feeling okay again and thinking, *I really did this, I helped her, I maybe sort of even saved her*—feeling pretty good in fact, letting Melissa hold on to his finger, until the policeman came and got them out of there.

Melissa smiled at the policeman all the way down.

It would be nice, Luke thought as he came down the ladder, if his mom had a baby someday. Like Melissa.

You never knew. Maybe she'd meet some guy.

It would be nice, he thought.

If she didn't, of course, that would be okay too.

It was good to know it really didn't matter.

PART VI

MAY 13, 1992
MORNING

9:45 A.M.

Peters dreamed that he and Mary dove off a pier into the sea. They were holding hands. They were naked and their bodies were twenty years old, smooth and firm. The sun was warm. They were getting away from someone or something which they did not fear exactly but which troubled them, and that was why they dove into the sea.

They swam through gentle waves around a short promontory, found sand beneath their feet, and again holding hands, began to emerge from the water.

Suddenly the beach became the streets of town and Mary realized she was naked. People were going on about their business as usual, not staring, but Mary was a modest woman and Peters was aware of her discomfort at running around town as god made her. He regretted leaving their clothes behind. They hadn't even any money to buy some.

He resolved the problem by stopping, turning toward Mary and embracing her.

"Now they can't see," he said.

She laughed. "George! We're in the middle of the street."

"That's the point," he said. "If we stand here long enough somebody will notice what nice people we are and how in love we are and get us some clothes eventually. Right?"

"Right," she said, and hugged him back.

"It all turns out eventually," he said.

And woke up.

He saw the covers on his bed and his body lying under them and saw that it was possible to move his hands. He dealt with that in amazement for a moment. He saw the hospital room and the flowers. And the people by his bed.

A woman with a bandaged head, seated in a chair. Nursing a pretty little baby.

Holding hands with another woman sitting beside him on the bed. The woman wore a light blue hospital gown the same as he did, but the woman was smiling at him, the first to notice he was awake.

And a boy dressed in jeans and a T-shirt standing by the window, staring out into the sunlight. The boy turned and glanced at Peters and then he smiled too.

With all these strangers around him smiling Peters had the god-damnedest urge to smile back at them.

And suddenly he remembered.

He looked over at the boy from the beach and remembered.

OFFSPRING

And then he did smile.
Hell, these weren't strangers.
They didn't *feel* like strangers.
"How'd I do?" he said.

Made in the USA
Columbia, SC
01 July 2024